The Two Elsies

The Original Elsie Classics

Elsie Dinsmore

Elsie's Holidays at Roselands

Elsie's Girlhood

Elsie's Womanhood

Elsie's Motherhood

Elsie's Children

Elsie's Widowhood

Grandmother Elsie

Elsie's New Relations

Elsie at Nantucket

The Two Elsies

Elsie's Kith and Kin

Elsie's Friends at Woodburn

Christmas with Grandma Elsie

Elsie and the Raymonds

Elsie Yachting with the Raymonds

Elsie's Vacation

Elsie at Viamede

Elsie at Ion

Elsie at the World's Fair

Elsie's Journey on Inland Waters

Elsie at Home

Elsie on the Hudson

Elsie in the South

Elsie's Young Folks

Elsie's Winter Trip

Elsie and Her Loved Ones

Elsie and Her Namesakes

The Two Elsies

Book Eleven of
The Original Elsie Classics

Martha Finley

CUMBERLAND HOUSE
NASHVILLE, TENNESSEE

The Two Elsies
by Martha Finley

Any unique characteristics of this edition:
Copyright © 2000 by Cumberland House Publishing, Inc.

Published by Cumberland House Publishing, Inc.,
431 Harding Industrial Drive, Nashville, Tennessee 37211.

Cover design by Bruce Gore, Gore Studios, Inc.
Photography by Dean Dixon Photography
Hair and Makeup by Calene Rader
Text design by Heather Armstrong

Printed in the United States of America
1 2 3 4 5 6 7 8 — 04 03 02 01 00

CHAPTER FIRST

Art is long, and Time is fleeting,
And our hearts, though stout and brave,
Still, like muffled drums, are beating
Funeral marches to the grave.

— *L*ONGFELLOW

IT WAS A LOVELY summer morning, glorious with sunlight and sweet with the fragrance of flowers and the song of birds.

The view from the bay window of the library of Crag Cottage, the residence of Mr. George Leland, architect and artist, was very fine, embracing, as it did, some of the most magnificent scenery on the banks of the Hudson.

The house stood very high, and from that window one might look north and south over wooded mountain, hill and valley, or east upon the majestic river and its farther shore.

The nearer view was of well-kept, though not extensive, grounds—a small flower garden and a lawn with a winding carriage way leading up the hill by a gradual ascent.

It was a pleasant place to sit even on a sunny summer morning—for a tall tree partially shaded the window without greatly obstructing the view. It was there the master of the house was usually to be found at this time of day with Evelyn, his only child, close at his side.

They were there now and were seated at a table covered with books and papers—he busied in drawing plans for a building, she equally so with her lessons.

But presently, at the sound of a deep sigh from her father, she glanced hastily at him.

He had dropped his pencil and was leaning back against the cushions of his easy chair with a face so wan and weary that she started up in alarm. Springing to his side exclaimed, "Dear papa, I am sure you are not well! Do stop working and lie down on the sofa. And won't you let me tell Patrick to go for the doctor when he has taken mamma to Riverside?"

"Yes, Evelyn, I think you may," he answered in low, feeble tones with a sad sort of smile, gently pressing the hand she had laid in his as he spoke. "It will do no harm for me to see Dr. Taylor, even should it do no good."

"What is that? Send for a doctor? Are you ill, Eric?" asked a lady who had entered the room just in time to catch his last sentence.

"I am feeling unusually languid, Laura," he replied. "Not much more so than I did yesterday. Perhaps it is only the heat."

"The heat!" she echoed. "Why, it is a delightful day! It is warm, to be sure, but not oppressively so."

"Not to you or me, perhaps, mamma," remarked Evelyn. "But we are well and strong, and poor papa is not."

"A holiday would do you good, Eric," the lady said, addressing her husband. "Come, change your mind and go with me to Riverside."

"My dear," he said, "I should like to go to gratify you, but really I feel quite unequal to the exertion."

"You need make none," she said. "You need only to sit quietly under the trees on the lawn. And I think you will find amusement in watching the crowd, while the fresh air, change of scene, and rest from the work you will not let alone when at home, will certainly be of great benefit to you."

He shook his head in dissent. "I should have to talk and listen—in short, to make myself agreeable. I have no right to inflict my companionship on Mrs. Ross's guests on any other condition, and all that would be a greater exertion than I feel fit to undertake, Laura."

"There was a time when you were willing to make a little exertion for my sake," she returned in a piqued tone. "But wives are not to expect the attention freely bestowed upon a sweetheart, and so I must go alone as usual."

"Mamma, what a shame for you to talk so to poor papa!" exclaimed Evelyn rather indignantly. "You know he is—"

"Hush, hush, Evelyn," said her father in a gently reproving tone. "Be respectful to your mother always, young lady."

"Yes, sir," returned the child, with a loving look into his eyes. Then to her mother, "I beg your pardon, I did not mean to be rude. But—" with a scrutinizing glance at the richly attired figure before her.

"Well?" laughingly interrogated the lady, as the child paused with a slight look of embarrassment and a heightened color.

"Nothing, mamma, only—"

"Something your correct taste disapproves about my attire?"

"Yes, mamma, your dress is very handsome—quite rich and bright enough for a ballroom, but—wouldn't a simpler, plainer one be more suitable for a lawn party?"

"Well, really!" was the laughing rejoinder. "The idea of such a child as you venturing to criticize her mother's taste in dress! You spoil her, Eric, making so much of her and allowing her to have and express an opinion on any and every subject. There, I must be going. I see Patrick is at the door with the carriage now. So good-bye, and don't overwork yourself, Eric."

"Mamma," Evelyn called after her, "Patrick is to go for the doctor after he leaves you."

"Oh, yes, I'll tell him," Mrs. Leland answered, and the next moment the carriage was whirling away down the drive.

"There, she is gone!" said Evelyn. "Oh, papa, when I am a woman I shall not marry unless I feel that I can always be content to stay with my husband when he is not able to go with me."

"But business may prevent him very often when sickness does not, and you may grow very weary of staying always at home," he said, softly smoothing her hair. Then, he bent to touch his lips to her smooth, white forehead and smile into the large, dark eyes lifted to his as she knelt at the side of his chair.

"No, no! Not if he is as dear and kind as you are, papa. But no other man is, I think."

"Quite a mistake, my dear. The world surely contains many better men than your father."

"I should be exceedingly angry if anyone else said that to me," she returned indignantly.

At that he drew her closer to him with a little pleased laugh. "We love each other very dearly, do we not, my darling?" he said, then sighed deeply.

"Indeed, we do!" she answered, gazing anxiously up into his face. "How pale and ill you look, papa! Do lie down and rest."

"Presently, when my work has progressed a little farther," he said, putting her gently aside, as he straightened himself and resumed his work.

Evelyn was beginning a remonstrance, but at the sound of the wheels upon the drive, she sprang to the window, exclaiming, "Can mamma be coming back already? She has perhaps changed her mind about attending the party. No," as she caught sight of the vehicle. "It is the doctor. I'm glad."

"Go. Receive him at the door, daughter, and show him in here," said Mr. Leland. "And as I desire a private interview, you may amuse yourself on the grounds while he stays."

"Yes, sir, and oh, I do hope he will be able to give you something that will make you well directly," the little girl replied, bestowing a look of loving anxiety upon her father and then hastening to obey his orders.

She received the physician at the front entrance with all the graceful courtesy of a refined lady, ushered him into the library. Then putting on a garden hat, she wandered out onto the grounds.

It was the month of roses, and they were to be found here in great variety and profusion. They bordered the walks, climbed the walls, and wreathed themselves about the pillars of the porches. The air was filled with their rich fragrance, which mingled with that of the honeysuckle, lilac, heliotrope, and migonette also to be found around the house and gardens.

Evelyn sauntered through the garden, pausing here and there to gather one and another of the most beautiful and sweet-scented of its floral treasures, arranging them in a bouquet for her father. Then, she crossed the lawn to an artistic little summerhouse built on the edge of the cliff, where it almost overhung the river.

The view from this spot was positively magnificent, extending for many miles and embracing some of the grandest scenery of that region. To Evelyn and her father, both dear lovers of the beauties of nature, it was a favorite resort.

Seating herself upon a rustic bench, she passed some moments in absorbed, delighted contemplation of the scene so familiar, yet ever new.

The thought that anything worse than a passing illness threatened her beloved father had not yet entered her youthful mind, and she sat there waiting for the departure of the physician as the signal that she might return to him.

From her earliest recollection he had been father and mother both to her. Mrs. Leland's time was too fully occupied with her onerous duties to society to allow her to bestow much attention upon her child.

Had the husband and father taken a like view of his responsibilities, Evelyn would have been left almost entirely to the care of the servants. But, to him the formation of his child's character and the cultivation of her mind and heart was a duty that outweighed all social claims, and to which even business might to some extent be sacrificed.

Nor was it a duty only, but also a delight. And so well was she rewarding his efforts that he found her, at thirteen, more companionable than her mother had ever been—taking enthusiastic interest in his professional work and sharing his aspirations for perfection therein and recognition as one of the foremost architects of his day.

In her esteem he had already distanced all close competitors. No one else could plan a house so well for comfort, convenience, and beauty combined. Also he was to her the very embodiment of all that was unselfish, good, and noble.

She thought, and truly, that her mother failed to appreciate him.

While Evelyn waited, the doctor subjected his patient to a thorough examination, not only feeling his pulse, listening to the beating of his heart, sounding his lungs, and looking at his tongue, but cross-questioning him closely, his face growing graver with every reply elicited.

"You have told me everything?" he finally inquired at length.

"Yes, I think so—every symptom that I can recall at this moment. And now, doctor, I want you to be equally frank with me. Tell me exactly what you think of my case."

"I cannot hold out any hope of recovery," was the unwilling reply. "But there actually is little, if any, immediate danger."

"You but confirm my own impressions," said Mr. Leland quietly. "But I would have a clearer understanding of your verdict. Do you mean that I may have years of invalidism before me, or that a few weeks or months must bring the end?"

"You really desire to know the worst, my dear sir?" returned the physician inquiringly, a look of deep sympathy on his kindly face.

"I do," was the calmly resolute reply. "Let me know the worst and face it in the strength God gives to His children according to their day."

"Then, my dear sir, I will be plain with you. Please bear in mind that I lay no claim to infallibility. I may err in judgment, but I see no reason to hope that your life on earth will be prolonged for more than three months at the most, and I much fear the end may come in less than half that time."

The doctor could not at first judge the full effect of his words for Mr. Leland sat with his face hidden in his hands.

For a moment a deathlike stillness reigned in the room. Then Dr. Taylor said, low and feelingly, "You are a Christian, my dear sir, and for you dying will be but going home to a brighter and better world."

"Yes," was the reply. "And your tidings would have no terrors for me were it not for those who must be left behind. But oh, the parting from helpless dear ones for whom my care and protection seems so necessary! That is the bitterness of death!"

"'Leave thy fatherless children, I will preserve them alive; and let thy widows trust in Me,'" quoted the physician in sympathizing tones.

"Yes. Yes. Thank God for that precious promise!" exclaimed Mr. Leland. "And you, doctor, for reminding me of it," he added, stretching out a hand to his kind comforter.

It was taken in a warm grasp and held for a moment, while others of the many sweet and comforting promises of God's Word were recalled to the mind of the sufferer to his great consolation.

"I would it were in my power," the doctor said at length, "to hold out to you any hope of restoration of health. I cannot do that, but I will write you a prescription which will, I trust, by God's blessing, give relief to some of the most distressing symptoms."

"Even partial relief will be most welcome," sighed the patient. "Ah, if I can but find strength for promised work!"

"Better let it alone and take what rest and ease you can," was the parting advice of the physician.

"What a long, long visit the doctor is paying!" Evelyn had said to herself several times before her eyes were gladdened with the sight of his carriage rolling away down the drive.

"At last!" she cried, springing to her feet and hurrying back to the house.

She found her father lying on a sofa—his face very pale, his eyes closed. She drew near on tiptoe, thinking he might have fallen asleep. But as she reached the side of his couch, he opened his eyes and took her hand, drawing her down to himself.

"My darling, my beloved child!" he whispered, putting his arm about her and holding her fast with tender caresses.

"What did the doctor say, papa?" she asked, nestling closer to him and laying her cheek to his. "Does he hope to make you well very soon?"

For a moment no reply came from her father's lips, and Evelyn, startled at her father's silence, suddenly raised her head and gazed earnestly, inquiringly into his face.

He smiled, a little sadly, and gently smoothed her hair back from her forehead. "I was thinking," he said, "of a text in the Psalm we read together this morning—'My soul, wait thou only upon God, for my expectation is from Him.' He and He only can make me well, daughter."

"Then why send for the doctor, papa?"

"Because God works by means. It pleases Him so to do, though it would be no more difficult to Him to accomplish His designs without. He has provided remedies, and I think it is His will that we should use them. At the same time we must ask His blessing upon them, feeling that without it they will be of no avail."

"Then you are to have some medicine, I suppose, my dear papa?"

"Yes, and to be out a good deal in the open air."

"Oh, then, won't you come out to the summer house and lie in the hammock there with me close beside you to wait on you?"

"Presently, but I must write a letter first," he said, putting her gently aside and resuming his seat at the writing table.

"Can't it wait till tomorrow, papa?" she asked. "You may feel stronger then."

"It is to be only a few lines to your Uncle Lester, and I want it to go by this afternoon's mail. That way, if possible, it may reach Fairview before they have arranged their plans for the summer. I want them to come here to spend the hot months. Should you like it?"

"Yes, indeed, papa! I've always been fond of Uncle Lester, as you know, and I quite fell in love with Aunt Elsie and the baby when he brought them to see us upon their return from Europe."

CHAPTER SECOND

How sudden do our prospects vary here!

It was the breakfast hour at Fairview. The young husband and wife chatted pleasantly over their coffee, omelet, and rolls, strawberries and cream, the principal subject of discourse being the expected trip to Nantucket in company with her mother, grandparents, and the rest of the family at Ion.

Lester and his Elsie had been there the previous evening, helping to celebrate the first anniversary of the marriage of Edward and Zoe, and had readily fallen in with the plans for the summer outing proposed by Captain Raymond.

"You will go with us, of course, Elsie and Lester?" their mother had said, several of the others eagerly echoing her words. They had answered that they knew of nothing to hinder and should be delighted to do so.

So that question seemed fully settled and now their talk was of needful preparations and arrangements for so long an absence from home, of the anticipated pleasures of the voyage and the proposed lengthened sojourn on Nantucket Island, including the sketching of the most attractive features of its scenery.

Young, healthy, in easy circumstances, entirely congenial in opinions and tastes, they were indeed a happy couple.

Lester was meeting with marked success in his chosen profession—had received only yesterday a large price for one of his paintings. And as Elsie and he were essentially one in all their interests, her joy was fully equal to his, if not greater.

In consequence, they were unusually happy this morning and life seemed very bright and beautiful before them.

They lingered over their meal and were just leaving the table when a servant came in with the morning's mail.

There were several newspapers and magazines—only one letter.

"From Eric, dear old boy! I was intending to write to him today," remarked Lester as he examined the superscription on the envelope.

"How nice, then, that his came just in time for you to answer it in yours," said Elsie. "I'll leave you to the enjoyment of it while I give my orders for the day," she added, turning from him toward the rear of the house as they left the breakfast room together.

"Yes, my dear, and when you have a spare moment to bestow upon your unworthy husband, you will find him on the veranda," he answered lightly, bending his steps in that direction.

Only a few minutes had passed when she sought him there, but what a change had come over him! All his happiness had forsaken him, his face was pale, and his eyes, as he turned them upon her, were full of anguish.

"Oh, Lester, my dear husband! What is it?" she cried, hastening to him and laying a hand tenderly upon his shoulder.

"Read," he said hoarsely, holding out the letter to her. Eric's letter, whose sad tidings seemed for the time to have driven away all joy and brightness of life.

Glancing down the page, Elsie read:

"My dear brother, will you come to me? I have sore need of you. For a year past I have felt my strength failing. For the last few months matters have grown worse, till my days and nights are filled with pain and unrest. And today I have learned that the time has come for me to set my house in order, for I am to 'die, and not live.' Nay, not so. I am to pass from the land of the dying to that blest world where death can never enter.

"My physician tells me it may possibly be three months ere I reach 'that bourne whence no traveler returns,' but that in all probability I shall arrive there in less than half that time.

"And there is much I would say to you, my brother, much in which I need your kind help. You will be coming north for the hot season. I would gladly have you, your sweet wife, and baby boy spend it here with us. To me it seems that there are few more pleasant places than this little home nest of ours high up on the rocky banks of the grand, old Hudson River. We have pure air and magnificent scenery and it will be most comforting to me to have your loved companionship as I go down into the valley of the shadow of death.

"Thank God, it is only a shadow, and I shall go down into it leaning on the strong arm of my beloved. Jesus will be with me to the very end.

"But I may be asking too much of my sweet sister Elsie. You and she have, perchance, formed other plans more congenial to your tastes and wishes. If so, let me not interfere with them. Consider my request withdrawn. Yet, shall I not have at least a sight of your loved faces ere I go hence to return no more?

"Lovingly, *Eric*."

Elsie could scarce see the signature through the fast-falling tears.

"The dear brother!" she sobbed. "But, oh, Lester, be comforted! His troubles and trials are almost over, the battle nearly ended, the victory well nigh won. And we know he will come off more than conqueror through Him that loved him!"

"Yes, I know. I know it, but he has been a dear brother to me, and, oh, how can I learn to live without him?" he answered, in tones quivering with emotion.

"'Twill only be for a time, love, and then you will be restored to each other, never to part anymore forever," Elsie said softly with her arm about her husband's neck. Her tears mingled with his own, and her sweet lips were pressed again and again to his cheek.

He folded her in a close embrace.

"My dear, sweet, precious comforter," he said. "I can never be unhappy while God spares me my own little wife."

"Nor I, while I have you, dearest," she responded with an added caress. "And we will go to poor Eric instead of with mamma and the rest to Nantucket."

"My sweet one, I could not ask so great a sacrifice from you," he said.

"I can hardly feel it to be such when I think of your poor brother, for is he not mine also? We will go to him instead and I know it will be with mamma's approval—grandpa's also. Ah, here they both come!" she exclaimed in a tone of satisfaction, as the Ion family carriage was seen approaching through the avenue.

In another moment it had drawn up before the entrance, and Mr. Dinsmore and his daughter alighted. With the quick eye of affection the mother at once noted the sadness of her daughter's countenance—of Lester's also—and scarcely had she exchanged the morning greeting with them ere she inquired the cause.

Lester silently handed her Eric's open letter.

Tears trembled in the soft, hazel eyes as she read.

In compliance with a mute request from Lester, she passed it on to her father.

There was a moment of silence after Mr. Dinsmore had finished reading, then the elder Elsie said in low, sympathizing tones, "My dears, you will go to him? Delightful as it would be to have you with us, I could not wish you to refuse such a request from one so near and dear."

"No, mamma dear, nor could we even think of refusing," answered her daughter quickly, glancing tenderly at her husband as she spoke and receiving a grateful, loving look in return.

"Certainly not," said Mr. Dinsmore. "But I see no reason why you should not accompany us on our voyage, spend a few days at Nantucket, and then go on to New York. Do you, Lester?"

"No, sir, and if my little wife approves of that plan, we will adopt it."

He turned inquiringly to her.

"I should like it very much," she said. "If you are quite sure it will not delay us too long," she added as an afterthought.

"No, scarcely at all, I think," returned Lester. "So we will consider that settled."

"Ah, I am very glad that we shall not lose your company altogether," Mrs. Travilla said. "And do not despair for your brother, Lester, for many very sick people have recovered, even after being given up by the doctors. We know, too, that with God nothing is impossible and that He is the hearer and answerer of prayer. We will unite our petitions on behalf of Eric, and if it shall be for God's glory and his good, he will be restored to health."

"Yes, mother, I have not a doubt of that," returned Mr. Leland. "Nor of my dear brother's safety in any case, as he is one who has lived the life of a Christian for years. I am sure dying grace will be given him for dying time—whenever that shall come."

"And well may you be," said Mrs. Travilla. "For not one of all God's promises ever fails. To each of His children, He has said, 'As thy days, so shall thy strength be.'"

"If you want to answer your letter by return mail, Lester, do not let us hinder you," said Mr. Dinsmore. "We are going to the village presently, and I will mail it for you, if you like."

"Thank you. Then I shall write at once," Lester replied, and he rose and left them.

"This change of plan will involve some change in your intended preparations, will it not, Elsie?" asked Mrs. Travilla.

"Not very much, mamma, as we are not likely to take part in any parties. I shall not need to have any new dresses made. Indeed, I think I have already a full supply of everything necessary or desirable in the way of dress for both baby and myself."

"Then you will be ready for the trip as soon as any of us?" her grandfather said inquiringly.

"Yes, sir, I could pack today and start this evening if desired to do so," she answered with a smile.

"We will not put you to the test," he said. "But we hope to sail next Tuesday."

CHAPTER THIRD

We all do fade as a leaf.

—*I*SAIAH *64:6*

A FORTNIGHT HAD PASSED since the day the doctor visited the dwellers in Crag Cottage. The June roses were blooming about it in even richer profusion than before. Tree and shrub and vine were laden with denser foliage. The place looked a very bower of beauty to the eyes of Lester and Elsie as the hack which had brought them from the nearest steamboat landing slowly wound its way up the hill on which the cottage stood.

On the vine-covered porch Eric lay in a hammock with his daughter, as usual, by his side.

Though losing flesh and strength day by day, he still persevered with his work. He had spent some hours over it this morning but was resting now. His cheek was fanned by the pure, sweet air from the mountain and river, and his eyes were feasting upon the beauties of the surrounding scenery. And ever and anon he turned a face full of fond, fatherly affection upon the face of the child he loved so well.

She was proving herself an excellent nurse for one of her age—never weary of waiting upon her loved patient. She was always striving to anticipate his every want and doing her best to entertain him and make him forget his pain.

She was talking of their expected guests.

"I am so glad they are coming, papa," she said. "I hope it will cheer you and do you much good to see your brother."

"And sister," he added with a faint smile. "Your Aunt Elsie is a very lovely and interesting woman."

"Yes, but I hope they will let me have my father to myself sometimes," she said, laying her cheek lovingly against the hand that was clasping hers. "I'm hardly willing to share you even with my dear Uncle Lester."

"No, not all the time," he responded. "We must have an hour alone together now and then. I should not like to be deprived of it any more than you."

She had lifted her head and was gazing toward the river. "Papa, I think they are here!" she exclaimed. "There is a carriage coming up the drive now."

"Ah, I hope so," he said, his pale cheek flushing with pleasure. Excitement lending him momentary strength, he hastily stepped from the hammock and with Evelyn went forward to greet and welcome the travelers as they alighted. The hack had now drawn up before the entrance.

Both Lester and Elsie were much moved at sight of their brother—so sadly changed from the vigorous man from whom they parted less than a year before.

Elsie had much ado to hide her emotion, and even Lester's voice was husky and tremulous as he returned Eric's greeting and made kind inquiries regarding his health.

"It is much the same as when I wrote you," Eric answered, holding fast to his brother's hand and gazing with a look of strong affection into his face. "And you are quite well?"

"Quite, thank you, but about yourself, Eric? Would it not be well to have other advice?"

"I believe there is none better than I have had, brother," Eric said. Then, turning to caress the little one in the nurse's arms, he cried, "What a fine little fellow! He's a truly beautiful child, sister Elsie. Ah, Lester, I rejoice that you have a son to keep up the family name. May he live to be a great blessing to you both!"

"How sweet and pretty he is!" Evelyn said, caressing him in her turn. "Aunt Elsie, shall I show you to your room?"

"If you please, my dear." They passed on into the house together, while Eric dropped exhausted into an easy chair and Lester took possession of another close at his side.

"You are very weak, Eric," he remarked in a tone of mingled affection and concern. "And I fear you suffer a great deal of pain."

"Yes, a great deal at times," he added with a joyous smile. "But I shall soon be in that land where there shall be no more pain, and the inhabitants shall not say 'I am sick.'"

"Please, don't speak of it, brother," said Lester hoarsely. "I must hope there are yet years of life in this world before you."

꙰ ꙰ ꙰ ꙰ ꙰

"What a very pleasant room, Evelyn. What a delightful prospect from that window looking toward the river!" Elsie exclaimed as Evelyn led the way into the spacious, airy apartment set apart for the occupation of herself and her husband during their stay.

"I think it is," Evelyn returned in a quiet tone. "That was the reason papa and I selected it for you. We have two other spare rooms, but this is the largest, and I think it has the loveliest views from its windows."

"Thank you, dear. Is your mamma well?"

"I suppose so. She was when we heard last, a day or two ago. She is at Newport, Aunt Elsie. She found herself so worn out, she said, with attending to the claims of society, that a trip to the seashore was quite a necessity. Do you put the claims of society before everything else, Aunt Elsie?"

"Indeed no," returned Elsie with a happy laugh. "I'm afraid I put them last on my list—husband, baby, mother, grandpa, brothers, and sisters—all come before society with me."

"So they shall with me when I'm a woman," said Evelyn with decision. "And papa shall always, always be first. I don't know how mamma can bear to be away from him so much, especially now when he is so weak and ailing. And I am quite mortified that she is not here to welcome you. She said she would be back in time but now writes that she finds Newport so delightful and the sea breezes doing her so much good that she can't bear to tear herself away just yet."

"Well, dear, as she is your mother and my sister, we will try not to criticize or find fault with her," responded Elsie in a gently soothing tone.

"No, I ought not," acknowledged Evelyn. "Papa never does—at least not to me. Mamma said she thought we could entertain you for a short time and we mean to do our best."

"Yes, dear child, but we must not allow your father to exert himself to that end. We did not come to be entertained, but to try to be of use to him."

"It was very kind," said Evelyn gratefully. "It must have been quite a sacrifice for you to leave that beautiful Nantucket so soon after arriving there. I know about it because we were there two summers ago and I could hardly bear to come away when our time was done."

"It is very pleasant there, but so it is here also," responded Elsie.

Evelyn looked much pleased. "I am glad you like it, Aunt Elsie," she said. "I think it the dearest spot on earth, but then it has always been my home."

"You are not just partial to it, Evelyn," Elsie said. "For it is a sweet spot."

"Thank you. Our dinner will be ready in about an hour from now, but don't take the trouble to dress. There will be no one but ourselves," Evelyn said, retiring from the room.

Elsie was not sorry to learn that her sister-in-law was absent from home, for though neither really disliked the other, they were not congenial. Their opinions, their tastes, their views of life—its pleasures and its duties—were so widely different that they could have but little in common.

A proud, self-important woman would have taken offense at the lack of hospitality and consideration shown her in the failure of the mistress of the house to be present with a welcome on her arrival, but such was not Elsie's character. She had but a humble opinion of her own importance and so very readily excused and overlooked the neglect.

But his wife's conduct was very mortifying to Eric, as he showed in his apology for her upon

Elsie's rejoining him and Lester on the porch where she had left them.

Elsie accepted his excuses very sweetly, assuring him that she expected to find much enjoyment in his, her husband's, and Evelyn's society, and she would have been very sorry indeed had Laura returned home for her sake before her visit to Newport was completed.

Evelyn, too, felt much chagrin on account of the lack of courtesy and hospitality in her mother's behavior toward these relatives esteemed by herself and her father as worthy of all honor. She made no remark about it to either of them, but tried most earnestly to fill her mother's place as hostess during her absence.

She was a very womanly little girl. She had a quaint, old-fashioned manner that Elsie thought quite charming. It was touching to see the devoted affection with which she hovered over and waited upon her sick father. She was seldom absent from his side for more than a few minutes at a time except when he sent her out for air and exercise.

Elsie usually accompanied her on her walks and drives, while Lester remained with his brother.

Eric seized these opportunities to open his heart to Lester in regard to the future of his only and beloved child, his one great anxiety in the prospect of death.

"I cannot leave her to her mother's care," he said with a sigh and a look of anguish. "It is a sad, indeed, a humiliating thing to say in regard to one's wife, but I have been sorely disappointed in my choice of a partner for life.

"We married for love, and she is very dear to me still, but our tastes and views are widely dissimilar.

She has no relish for the quiet pleasures of home, finds duties of a wife and mother extremely irksome, and is not content unless living in a constant whirl of excitement—a never-ending round of pleasure parties, balls, concerts, and other life's most fashionable amusements.

"I cannot join her in it, and so, for years past, we have gone our separate ways.

"Evelyn, as her mother has no time to bestow upon her, has been left almost entirely to me. I have earnestly striven to train her up to a noble Christian womanhood, to cultivate her mind and heart, and to give her a taste for far higher pleasures than those to be found in the giddy whirl of fashionable follies.

"I think I have reasonably succeeded to some extent, but she is so young, that, of course, much of the work yet remains to be done. Laura is not the person to carry it on. Also, I think, she would not covet the task.

"Lester, if you will undertake her guardianship and receive her into your family to be brought up under the influence of your lovely wife and mother-in-law, I shall die happy. Would it be asking too much, my dear brother?"

"You could not ask too much of me, Eric," Lester said with emotion. "And if my Elsie is willing, it shall be as you wish."

Eric expressed his thanks and his hope that Elsie would not object.

"My darling will not be a troublesome charge," he said. "She has her faults, of course, but they are not the kind to make her a disagreeable inmate of your family. Her admiration of her Aunt Elsie is so great that doubtless she will yield readily to her wishes and study to be like her in her loveliness of character and manners."

"Yes, Evelyn is a child any father might be proud of," assented Lester. "Surely her mother cannot help being fond of her, and you would not wish to separate them, Eric?"

Eric looked much disturbed. For a moment he seemed lost in thought. Then he said, "I cannot tell just what Laura will do. She certainly must have some affection for our child, but not enough, I fear, to make her willing to resign any pleasure for her sake. I think she will not care for a settled home when I am gone but, I fear, will spend her time in flitting about from one fashionable resort to another. In that case, Evelyn would be only a burden and care to her—one she will probably be glad to get rid of. I see plainly that it could be for neither your happiness nor Laura's to attempt to live together, but perhaps you would be willing to receive her as a guest occasionally for a short time?"

"Certainly," Lester said. "And I would be only so happy to assist her financially, if necessary."

"Thank you for the generous offer," returned Eric gratefully. "But there will be no need to trespass upon your kindness in that way. Laura has some money of her own, and her proportion of mine will make her very comfortable. The remainder will be sufficient to clothe and educate Evelyn and give her a moderate income afterward for the rest of her life if it is not lost in any way. That she will not be robbed of it in her minority I feel certain, having been so fortunate as to secure you for my executor," he added with an affectionate glance and smile.

"I shall certainly do the best I can to take care of it for her," Lester said, his voice a little unsteady with the thought that these were his brother's dying wishes to which he was listening. "But I am not a business man, and—"

"I am quite willing to trust your good sense, your honesty, and your love for your niece," interrupted Eric, hearing the approaching footsteps of Elsie and his daughter.

Evelyn's wish that she might sometimes have her father to herself was gratified. Lester and Elsie were thoroughly considerate, and almost every day they went out together for an hour or more, leaving the little girl to perform the duties of nurse.

Then there was an exchange of confidences and endearments such as was not indulged in the presence of any third person. Eric used the occasion to give his darling much tender and wise fatherly counsel—such that he thought might be of use when he would no longer be at her side.

He did not tell her of the trial that was drawing so near, of the parting that would rend her heart. However, she more than suspected it, as she saw her father day by day grow a little weaker, paler, and thinner.

But the very idea was so terrible that she put it resolutely from her, and she thought and talked hopefully of the time when he would be well again.

He could not bear to crush the hope that made her so bright and happy. But he spoke often to her of the blessedness of those who sleep in Jesus. And he made her read to him the passage of Scripture which tells of the glories and bliss of heaven—of the inheritance of the saints in light—the things which "eye hath not seen nor ear heard, neither the heart of man conceived"—the things that God hath prepared for them that love Him, for them "who have washed their robes and made them white in the blood of the Lamb."

CHAPTER FOURTH

Never morning wore
To evening, but some heart did break.

— *T*ENNYSON

LAURA LINGERED AT Newport for several weeks after the arrival of Lester and Elsie at Crag Cottage, so that the brothers had abundance of time and opportunity for private talks and business arrangements and for Evelyn to practice the role of hostess.

When at last she did reach home, she was greatly shocked at the change in her husband and she heaped reproaches upon poor Evelyn for not giving her more faithful reports of his condition.

"Mamma," said the little girl, "I did write you that he was getting weaker and weaker, that he was no longer able to walk or even drive out, and that he had wakeful, restless nights. I thought you would certainly want to come to him when you heard that. But don't worry, Dr. Taylor has changed the medicine and I hope he will soon be better now."

"No, he won't. He'll not live a month!" she exclaimed angrily. Then, glancing at Evelyn's pale, terror-stricken face, she said, "Pshaw, child! Don't be frightened. I did not really mean it. I dare say we shall have him about again in a few weeks."

"Mamma, what do you really think?" asked the little girl, clasping her hands and gazing into her mother's face with a look of agonized entreaty. "I know you believe in deceiving people sometimes when you think it for their good—for I have heard you say so. But I want to know the truth, even if it breaks my heart."

"I'm not a doctor, Evelyn," returned her mother coldly. "I can judge only from appearances, which are as visible to you as to me. Besides, what is the use of my giving my opinion, since you choose to believe I am capable of intentionally deceiving you?"

With her last words she sailed from the room, leaving Evelyn quite alone in the parlor where the conversation had taken place.

Evelyn sat like one stunned with a heavy blow. Could it be that her father was dying—the dear father who was all the world to her? Oh, what would life be worth without him? How could she go on living? How soon would the dread parting come? How many more days or hours might she spend in his dear companionship? Ah, those precious hours were fast slipping away—every moment spent away from his side was a great loss. She would go to him at once.

She started up, but dropped into her seat again. Mamma was with him, and just now she would rather avoid her society.

Covering her face with her hands, she sat silently thinking. She went over and over again in her imagination all that had passed between her father and herself during the last few weeks. She recalled their conversations—especially every word he had addressed to her bearing upon her future. She remembered all his loving counsels, his fatherly exhortations to lean upon God in every time of trial and perplexity and to carry every sorrow, anxiety, and care to the Lord Jesus in unwavering confidence that there she would find never-failing sympathy, comfort, and help.

Now for the first time it struck her that thus he was trying to prepare her to do without him—the earthly parent who had been hitherto the confidant of all her childish griefs, perplexities, hopes, joys, and fears. With that thought, her fear and conviction deepened that he was indeed passing away to that bourne whence no traveler returns.

Tears were stealing between the slender fingers and low, deep sobs were shaking her slight frame, when a hand was gently laid on her shoulder. A sweet-toned voice asked in tender accents, "What is it, Evelyn, dear?"

"Oh, Aunt Elsie!" cried the little girl, lifting a tear-stained face. "You will tell me the truth! Is my dear papa—no, no, I can't say it—but oh, do you think we may hope he will soon be well again?"

"My dear child," Elsie said in quivering tones as she seated herself and, putting an arm about the girl's waist, drew her close with a tender caress. "He is very ill, but 'while there is life there is hope,' for with God all things are possible."

"Oh, I know—I understand what that means!" cried Evelyn in anguished accents. "He is dying! My dear, dear father!"

"My poor child. My poor, dear child!" Elsie said, her tears falling fast. "I can feel for you, for it is not very long since I stood by the deathbed of a dear father. Flesh and heart fail in such a trial, but look to Jesus for help and strength to endure, and He will sustain and comfort you as He did me."

"I can never, never bear it!" sobbed Evelyn, hiding her face on Elsie's shoulder. "And papa— oh, how dreadful for him to have to go away all alone! I wish I could go with him."

"That cannot be, dear, but he will not go alone. 'Yea, though I walk through the valley of the shadow of death, I will fear no evil; for Thou art with me.' Jesus will be with him and he will need no one else."

"Yes, I know, and I am glad for him. But, oh, who will be with me when he is gone? Mamma is seldom at home and cares nothing for having me with her."

"God will raise up friends and companions for you, my dear, and if you seek the Lord Jesus, He will be to you a Friend indeed—One who sticketh closer than a brother or father, or any earthly creature, and a Friend who will never die, never leave or forsake you."

For some moments there was silence in the room, broken only by Evelyn's low sobs. But at length she spoke in trembling, tearful tones, "Will the angels come and carry him to heaven, Aunt Elsie, as they did the poor beggar, Lazarus, that the Bible tells us all about?"

"Yes, dear, I believe they will," Elsie answered, tenderly smoothing the child's hair. "And I think they will be full of joy for him, because he will be done with all the pains, the troubles, and the trials of earth, He will be going to be forever with the Lord. I believe they will carry him home with songs of gladness. And oh, what a welcome he will receive when he enters the gates of the Celestial City! The Bible tells us 'Precious in the sight of the Lord is the death of his saints,' and that 'He shall see of the travail of His soul and be satisfied.' It tells us that His love for His people exceeds in depth and tenderness that of a mother for her child. Then, how must He rejoice over each one of His ransomed ones as He takes them in His arms and bids them welcome to the blissful mansions He has prepared for them?"

"Yes, I shall be glad for papa. But, oh, Aunt Elsie, what can I do without him?"

"God will help and comfort you, dear child. He will be your father," Elsie said with emotion. "'A father to the fatherless and a judge of the widows is God in His holy habitation.'"

"It is a very sweet promise," said Evelyn. "Aunt Elsie, I wish I knew that was a true, a real occurrence—that story of the rich man and Lazarus. Then I should be quite sure that angels do come and carry home Christians when they die, and that they will come for papa. But some people say it is only a parable."

"But the Bible does not say so," returned Elsie. "Jesus narrates it as a real occurrence, and I believe it was. Nothing has ever happened in any world that He has not seen and known. Therefore, he was perfectly competent to tell about the life and death of any man and also of his experiences after death. So I think, dear child, you may take all the comfort you can find in believing it a narrative of an actual occurrence.

"Evelyn, I remember something that may perhaps give you comfort as additional proof that angels do carry home the souls of God's children from earth to heaven. I heard an old minister—a man whose honest word I should credit as entirely as the evidence of my own senses—tell it to my mother.

"He said that when he was a boy at home on his father's farm, he and his brother were one evening out in a meadow attending to their horses. Some short distance from them was the dwelling of an old elder—a remarkably devoted Christian man, who always had family worship morning and evening, and always, on those occasions, sang one of two hymns.

"On this particular evening the lads, while busy in the meadow, were surprised to hear sounds as of a number of voices singing one of the elder's two tunes—I have forgotten now which it was—but the sounds came nearer and nearer from the direction of the elder's house and, to the great wonder and astonishment of the lads, passed above their heads.

"They heard the voices in the air, but saw nothing of the singers. Afterward they learned that the good old man had died just at that time."

"How strange," said Evelyn in an awe-struck tone. "Oh, Aunt Elsie, if I could hear their song of joy over papa, I should not grieve quite so much." The door opened and Laura looked in.

"Evelyn," she said in a piqued tone, "your father wants you. It actually seems that you, a mere child, are more necessary to him than his own wife. He would see you alone for a few minutes."

Silently, for her heart was too full for speech, Evelyn withdrew herself from Elsie's arms and hastened to obey the summons at once.

CHAPTER FIFTH

Gone before
To that unknown and silent shore.

— Charles Lamb

Mr. Leland, lying pale and languid upon his couch, was listening intently for the approaching footsteps of his child.

As she stole softly in, fearful of disturbing him, he lifted his head slightly and greeted her with a tender, pitying smile and a feebly outstretched hand.

"My darling," he whispered, drawing her to him. "My poor darling, so they have told you? I have tried to spare you the bitter truth as long as I could. It is bitter to you, love, and to me for your sake, yet the will of God be done. He knows and will do what is best for us both."

Evelyn was making a very determined effort at self-control for his dear sake, that she might not disturb him with the knowledge that her very heart was breaking.

"Papa," she said with a vain endeavor to steady her tones, "dear, dearest papa, you will surely get well, for I pray day and night to God to cure you. Have you not taught me that He is the hearer and answerer of prayer, that He loves us, and that He is able to do everything?"

"Yes, dear daughter, and it is all true, but His thoughts are not our thoughts. He may see best to take me now to the heavenly home toward which you, too, I hope, are traveling—best for you as well as for me."

"Oh, papa, how can it be best for me, when you are such a help to me in going that road—the only help I have?"

"He is able to raise up other and better helpers for you, dearest, and He Himself will be the best of all. Perhaps it is to draw you nearer to Himself that He is taking away the earthly father upon whom you have been accustomed to lean."

Mr. Leland's voice faltered with the last words. The exertion of talking so much had exhausted his feeble frame, and closing his eyes, he lay lifting up silent petitions for his child.

Evelyn thought he slept, and lest she should disturb him, forcibly repressed her inclination to relieve her overburdened heart by sobs and sighs.

She remained close at his side, gently fanning him, for the day was oppressively hot.

But presently he opened his eyes and fixed them upon her face with a long look of tenderest love and sympathy—a look that impressed itself indelibly upon her memory. This look was often, in after years, dwelt upon with feelings of strangely mingled joy and grief.

"My darling," he murmured at length, so low that her quick ear scarce caught the words, "my precious child, I leave you to the care of Him who is Father of the fatherless. I have been pleading with Him for you, pleading His promise to those who trust in Him. He has promised, 'I will be a God to thee and to thy seed after thee.' It is an everlasting covenant and shall never fail you. Seek Him, my darling. Seek Him with all your heart, and He will be your God forever and ever—your Guide even unto death."

"I will, papa, I will," she whispered, pressing her quivering lips to his cheek.

The end did not come that day. For another week the loved sufferer lingered in pain and weakness, borne with Christian fortitude and resignation.

For the most part his mind was both clear and calm, the joy of the Lord his strength and stay. Yet were there moments when doubts and fears assailed him.

"What is it, dear brother?" Elsie asked one day, seeing a troubled look upon his face.

"'How many are mine iniquities and sins,'" he answered softly. "'Mine iniquities are gone over mine head, as a heavy burden they are too heavy for me.'"

"But 'He was wounded for our transgressions, He was bruised for our iniquities; the chastisement of our peace was upon Him; and with His stripes we are healed,'" quoted Elsie.

"Oh, bless the Lord 'who forgiveth all thine iniquities.'"

"Yes," he said. "But I am so vile, so sinful—it seems utterly impossible that I ever can be pure in His sight who is 'of purer eyes than to behold evil, and cannot look on iniquity.'"

"'The blood of Jesus Christ his Son cleanseth us from all sin,'" quoted Elsie in tones of sympathy.

"'Thou shalt call His name Jesus, for He shall save His people from their sins.'

"'This Man, because he continueth ever, hath an unchangeable priesthood. Wherefore He is able to save them to the uttermost that come unto God by Him, seeing He ever liveth to make intercession for them.'

"'Who gave Himself for us, that He might redeem us from all iniquity.'

"'Let Israel hope in the Lord; for with the Lord there is mercy, and with Him is plenteous redemption. And He shall redeem Israel from all his iniquities.'"

"Blessed words!" he exclaimed, the cloud lifting from his brow. "Blessed, blessed words! I will doubt and fear no more. I will trust His power to save. His imputed righteousness is mine and covered with the spotless robe I need not fear to enter the presence of the King of kings."

Some hours later the messenger came for him. Whispering, "All is peace, peace, unclouded peace," the dying saint fell asleep in Jesus.

Gently, tenderly Lester closed the sightless eyes, saying in moved tones, "Farewell, brother beloved! Thank God the battle's fought, the victory won!"

And now Evelyn, who had been for hours close at her father's side, waiting upon him, smoothing his pillow, moistening his lips, gazing with yearning tenderness into his eyes, drinking in his every word and look while displaying a power of self-control amazing to see in a child of her years, burst into a passion of tears and sobs, pressing her lips again and again to the brow, the cheek, the lips of the dead — those pale lips that for the first time failed to respond to her loving caresses.

However, with a wild shriek, the new-made widow went into strong hysterics, and, resuming her self-control, the little girl left the dead to wait upon and console the living parent.

"Mamma, dearest mamma," she said in quivering tones, putting her arms about her mother, "think how blest he is. The angels are even now carrying him home with songs of gladness to be forever with the Lord, and he will never be sick or in pain any more."

"But what is to become of me?" sobbed her mother. "I cannot do without him even if you can. You couldn't have loved him half so well as I did, or you would never take his loss so quietly."

"Oh, mamma!" cried the child, her tone speaking deeply wounded feeling. "If you could know how I loved him—my dear, dear father! Oh, why am I left behind? Why could I not go with him?"

"And leave your mother alone!" was the reproachful rejoinder. "But you always loved him best. You never cared particularly for me, and never will, I suppose," she added, going into an even stronger paroxysm than before.

"Oh, mamma, don't!" cried Evelyn in very sore distress. "I love you dearly, too, and you are all I have left." She threw her arm about her mother's neck as she spoke but was thrust impatiently aside.

"You are suffocating me, can't you see it? Help me to bed in the next room, and call Hannah. She perhaps will have sense enough to apply restoratives."

Both Lester and Elsie had come to her aid, and the former, taking her in his arms, carried her to the bed, while Evelyn hastened to call the nurse who had for the past week or two assisted in the care of him who now no longer needed anything but the last, sad offices.

Laura's grief continued to be very violent in its manifestations, yet did not hinder her from taking an absorbing interest in the preparation of her own and Evelyn's mourning garments. She was careful that they should be of the deepest black, the finest quality, the most fashionable cut—to all of which the bereaved child, a silent and undemonstrative mourner, was supremely indifferent. Her mother noted it with surprise, for Evelyn was a child of decided opinions and wont to be fastidious about her attire.

"Flounces on this skirt, I suppose, miss? How many?" asked the dressmaker.

"Just as mamma pleases. I do not care in the least," returned Evelyn.

"Why, Eva, what has come over you?" queried her mother. "It is something new for you to be indifferent in regard to your dress."

"You are the only one I care to please now, mamma," replied the little girl in tremulous tones. "I think there is no one else likely to be interested in the matter."

Laura was touched. "You are a good child," she said. "And I think you may very well trust everything to my taste. It is considered to be excellent by my friends and acquaintances."

With thoughtfulness beyond her years, Evelyn presently drew her mother aside out of earshot of the dressmaker and whispered, "Mamma, dear, don't put too much expense on me. You know there is no one to earn money for us now."

"No, but he cannot have left us poor," rejoined the mother. "I know his business has paid very well indeed for years past. And of course his wife and child inherit all he has left."

"I do not know! I do not care!" cried Evelyn, hot tears streaming from her eyes. "What is money without papa to help us enjoy it?"

"Something that is very convenient, indeed, absolutely necessary, to have in this practical world, as you will know when you are older and wiser," returned her mother with some severity of tone. Evelyn's words had seemed to her like a reproach and an insinuation that Eric's daughter was a deeper and more sincere mourner for him than his widow.

Such was truly the fact but she was by no means ready to admit it. And she loved him, perhaps, as well as she was capable of loving anyone but herself. Since her return home, she had been too much occupied with his critical condition, and then his death, to give a thought to the state of his affairs or the disposition to be made of his property.

True, she had little cause for anxiety in regard to these things, knowing that he had no financial entanglements. She had heard him say on more than one occasion that whatever he might possess at the time of his death would be left to his wife and child. Yet, had she been an unloving wife, queries, hopes, and fears in regard to the amount he was leaving her would have found some place in her thoughts.

And now that Evelyn had in a manner opened the subject, they did so. She was no longer absorbed in her grief. It was present with her still, but her thoughts were divided between it on the one hand and her mourning and future prospects on the other.

It now occurred to her that Evelyn, being under age and also heir to some property, must have a proper guardian.

"That should be left to me," she said to herself. "I am quite capable—her natural guardian, too, and I trust he has not associated anyone else with me. It would be too provoking, for he would be forever interfering in my plans and wishes for the child."

She waited until the day after that on which the body was laid away in its last resting place. Then, finding herself alone with her brother-in-law, said to him, "I want a little talk with you, Lester, for it is time for me to be arranging my plans. As you were with your brother for some weeks before his death, I presume you can tell me all about his affairs. Did he make a will?"

"He did, leaving his entire estate to his wife and child," replied Lester in a grave but kindly tone.

"One third to me and two to her, I suppose?"

"Yes, but I think he said you would be the richer of the two, having some property of your own."

"That is quite correct. I am appointed executrix and guardian to Evelyn, of course?"

"No," Lester replied with some hesitation, for he saw that she would be ill-pleased with the arrangements Eric had made. "At the earnest solicitation of my brother, I consented to become his executor and the guardian of his child."

Laura did not speak for a moment, but her eyes flashed and her cheek paled with anger. "Ah, I might have known it," she hissed at length. "Had I not been the most innocent and unsuspicious of women, I should have known better than to leave him for weeks to the wiles of designing relatives, when, too, his mind was weakened by disease."

"His mind was perfectly clear and strong from first to last, Laura," returned Lester mildly. "And you are greatly mistaken in supposing I had anything to gain by agreeing to his wishes, or that I was at all covetous of either office."

"Pardon me," she sneered. "But if you do not receive a percentage for your trouble, you will be the first executor I ever heard of who did not."

"I shall not accept a cent," he retorted with some slight indignation in his tones.

"We shall see. Men can change their minds as well as women. But surely I am associated with you in the guardianship of Evelyn?"

"According to her father's will I am her sole guardian," said Lester.

"It is too much. I am the child's natural guardian and shall contest my rights if necessary," returned Laura defiantly, and with the last word she rose and left the room.

Elsie, entering the parlor a moment later, found her husband pacing to and fro with a disturbed and anxious air.

"What is the matter?" she asked. He answered with an account of his interview with Laura.

"How strange!" she exclaimed. "Her love for her husband cannot have been very deep and strong if she is so ready to oppose the carrying out of his dying wishes. But do not let it trouble you, Lester. She is venting her anger in idle threats and will never proceed to the length of contesting the will in a court of law."

"I trust not," he said sighing. "Ah, me! If my poor brother had but made a wiser choice."

In the library, whither Mrs. Laura Leland bent her steps on her sudden exit from the parlor, Evelyn was sitting in her father's vacant chair. Her elbow was resting on the table, her cheek in her hand, her eyes on the carpet at her feet, while her sad thoughts traveled back over many an hour spent there in the loved companionship of the dear and departed one.

She looked up inquiringly on her mother's abrupt entrance and noted with surprise the flush of her cheek and the angry light in her eyes.

"Ah, here you are!" said Laura. "Pray, were you let into the secret of the arrangements made in my absence, daughter?"

"What arrangements, mamma?" asked the little girl wonderingly.

"In regard to your guardianship, and the care of the property left by your father."

"No, mamma, I never knew or thought anything about those things. Must I have a guardian? Why should I be under the control of anyone but you?"

"Yes, why indeed? I would not have believed it of your father! But he has actually left you to the sole guardianship of your Uncle Lester. You may well look astonished," she added, noting the expression of Evelyn's face. "I feel that I am robbed of my own natural right to my child."

"You need not, mamma. I shall obey you just the same, of course, for I know nothing can release me from the obligation to keep the fifth commandment. So do not, I beg you, blame papa."

With quite a quiver of pain the young voice pronounced that loved name!

"No, I blame your uncle. For no doubt he used undue influence with Eric while his mind was enfeebled by illness. And I blame myself also for leaving my husband to that influence. But I little thought he was so ill—so near his end. Nor did I suspect his brother of being so designing a man."

"Mamma, you are quite mistaken in regard to both," exclaimed Evelyn in a pained, indignant tone. "Uncle Lester is not at all a designing person, and papa's mind was not in the least enfeebled by his illness."

"No, of course not. It can not be doubted that a child of your age is far more capable of judging than a woman of mine," was the sarcastic rejoinder.

"Mamma, please do not speak so unkindly to me," entreated the little girl, unbidden tears springing to her eyes. "You know you are all I have now."

"No, you have your dear Uncle Lester and Aunt Elsie, and I foresee that they will soon steal your heart entirely away from your mother."

"Mamma, how can you speak such cruel words to me?" cried Evelyn. "I would not hurt you so for all the world."

Chapter Sixth

Farewell; God knows when we shall meet again.

—*S*HAKESPEARE

LAURA SAID NO MORE about breaking the will, but her manner toward Lester and Elsie was so cold and repellant that they were not sorry that she shut herself up in her own room during the greater part of each day while they and she remained at Crag Cottage.

Had they consulted only their own inclination, they would have taken their own departure immediately after seeing Eric laid in his grave. But Lester's duties as executor and guardian made it necessary for them to stay on for some weeks.

The cottage was a part of Evelyn's portion of the estate, but Laura was given the right to make it her home so long as she remained Eric's widow.

Laura knew this, having read the will, but as that instrument made no mention of Eric's desire that his daughter should reside with her guardian, she was not aware of that fact. And, feeling well nigh certain that it would rouse her anger and total opposition, Lester dreaded making the disclosure.

So, while perplexing himself with the question of how best to approach her on the subject, he found among his brother's personal papers a sealed letter addressed to her.

Calling Evelyn, he put it into her hand, bidding her to carry it to her mother.

Half an hour later the little girl was again at his side, asking in tearful tones, "Uncle Lester, must mamma and I be separated?"

He was in the library seated before a table and seemed very busy over a pile of papers laid thereon, but pushing back his chair, he threw his arm around her waist and drew her to his knee.

"No, my dear child, not necessarily," he said, softly caressing her hair and cheek. "Your mother will be made welcome at Fairview if she sees fit to go with us."

"But she wants to stay here and keep me with her. And it's my home, you know, the dear home where everything reminds me of—papa. Will you not let me stay?"

"Do you really wish it, Evelyn? Do you not desire to carry out the dying wishes of the father you loved so dearly?"

"Yes, uncle," she said, the tears stealing down her cheeks. "But—perhaps he wouldn't care now, and mamma is sorely distressed at the thought of our separation. And—and it hurts me, too, for she is my mother, and I have no father now—or brother, or sister."

"You must let me be a father to you, my poor, dear child," he said in moved tones as he drew her closer. "I will do my utmost to fill his place to you, and I hope you will come to me always with your troubles and perplexities, feeling the same assurance of finding sympathy and help that you did in carrying them to him."

"Oh, thank you!" she responded. "I think you are a dear, kind uncle and very much like papa. You remind me of him very often in your looks and words and ways."

"I am glad to hear you say so," he answered. "I had great admiration for that dear brother, and for his sake, as well as her own, I am very fond of his little daughter. But now, about this question—I shall not compel your obedience to your father's wishes—at least not for the present. I shall leave the decision to your own heart and conscience. Take a day or two to think over the matter, and let me hear your decision.

"In the meantime, if you can persuade your mamma to go with us to Fairview, that will make it all very smooth and easy for you."

"Thank you, dear uncle," she said, as he released her and turned to his work again. "I will go now and try what I can do to induce mamma to accept your kind invitation. Please excuse me for having interrupted you when you were so busy."

"I am never too busy to attend to you, Evelyn," he returned in a kindly tone. "Come freely to me whenever you will."

Crossing the hall, Evelyn noticed the carriage of an intimate friend of her mother drawn up before the entrance.

"Mrs. Lang must be calling on mamma," she said to herself. Pausing near the half-open parlor door, she saw them sitting side by side on a sofa, conversing in earnest, though subdued tones.

The call proved a long one. Evelyn waited with what patience she might, vainly trying to interest herself in a book—her thoughts much too full of her own near future to allow her doing so.

At last Mrs. Lang took her departure, and Evelyn, following her mother into her bedroom, gave a detailed account of her most recent interview with her uncle.

"Mamma, dear, you will go with us, will you not?" she concluded persuasively.

"No, I shall not!" was the angry rejoinder. "Spend weeks and months in a dull, country place with no more enlivening society that that of your uncle and aunt? Indeed, no! You will have to choose between them and me. If you love them better than you do your own mother, elect, by all means, to forsake me and go with them."

"Mamma," remonstrated poor Evelyn, tears of wounded feeling in her eyes, "it is not a question of loving you or them best, but of obeying my father's dying wish."

For a moment Mrs. Leland seemed to be silently musing. Then, she said, "I withdraw my request, Evelyn. I have decided upon new plans for myself, and I should prefer you to go with your uncle. You needn't look hurt, child. I'm sure it is what you have seemed to desire anyway."

"Mamma," said the little girl, going up to her, standing by the side of her easy chair, and gazing down beseechingly into her eyes, "why will you persist in speaking so doubtfully of my love for you? It hurts me, mamma. It almost breaks my heart, especially now that you are all I have left."

"Well, there, you need not fret. Of course, I know you must have some natural affection for your mother," returned Laura carelessly.

"Here, sit down on this stool at my feet, and you shall hear about my change in plans.

"Mrs. Lang called to tell me they are going to Europe—will sail in a fortnight—and to ask me to accompany them. I have accepted the invitation. You were included in it also, but I shall have less care if I leave you behind. And though I always intended that you should have the trip some day, I think it much the wiser plan to defer it for a few years till you are old enough to appreciate and make the best use of all the advantages.

"Besides, your uncle being your guardian, his consent would have to be gained, and I have no mind to stoop to ask it."

"Mamma, I am satisfied to stay," said Evelyn. "I should be very loath to add to your cares or lessen in any way your enjoyment."

It was with no slight feeling of relief that Lester and Elsie heard of this new determination on the part of their sister-in-law—for her present behavior toward them thus far had been such as to make her presence in their home anything but desirable.

With an aching heart Evelyn watched and aided in the preparations for her mother's departure, which would take place some weeks earlier than her own and that of her uncle and aunt.

Naturally quiet and undemonstrative, she usually kept her feelings locked up within herself. In consequence, she was sometimes accused by her mother of being coldhearted and indifferent.

Yet, as the day of separation drew near, Laura grew more affectionate toward her child than she had ever been before.

That was pure joy for Evelyn, but made the parting more bitter when it came. Mother and child wept in each other's arms, and Evelyn whispered with a bursting sob, "Oh, mamma, if you would only give it up and go with us!"

"Nonsense, child! It is quite too late for that now," returned Laura, giving her a last embrace and hurrying into the carriage that was to convey her to the depot. She was to travel by rail to New York City and from there take the steamer for Europe.

Lester went with her to the city—to see her safe on board the vessel, leaving his wife and child behind. Elsie's tender heart was full of pity for Evelyn—now robbed of both parents and left quite lonely and forlorn.

"Dear child, be comforted," she said, embracing her tenderly as the carriage disappeared from sight down the drive. "You have not been deserted by your best Friend. 'When my father and mother forsake me, then the Lord will take me up.'

"And be assured your uncle and I will do all in our power to make you happy. I am not old enough to be a mother to you, but let me be an older sister.

"And I will share my own dear mother with you," she added with a sweet and bright smile. "Everybody loves mamma, and she has a heart big enough to mother all the motherless children with whom she comes in contact."

"Thank you, dear Aunt Elsie," Evelyn responded, smiling through her tears, then hastily wiping them away. "I am sure I shall love your mamma and be very grateful if she will count me among her children while my own mamma is so far away. Sure, too, that I shall be as happy with you and Uncle Lester as I could be anywhere without papa."

"I hope so, indeed," Elsie said. "And that you will find pleasant companions in the Ion young people.

Both my sister, Rosie, and Lulu Raymond must be quite near your age. You probably come in between them, I should think."

"And I suppose they are very nice girls?" remarked Evelyn inquiringly.

"I think they are," said Elsie. "They have their faults like any of the rest of us, but they have many good qualities, too."

Desirous to divert Evelyn's thoughts from her sorrows, Elsie went on to give a lively description of Ion and a slight sketch of the character and appearance of each member of the family, doing full justice to every good trait and touching but lightly upon faults and failings. Evelyn proved an interested listener. Fairview and then Viamede came under a similar review, and Elsie told the story of her mother's birth and her infant years passed in that lovely spot. Then she told of her honeymoon and of the visits paid by the family in later days to the beautiful southern home.

"What a very sweet lady your mamma must be, Aunt Elsie," Evelyn remarked in a pause in the narrative. "I am glad I shall see and know her."

"Yes, dear, you well may be," Elsie responded with a happy smile. "'None knew her but to love her.' I know of none that can live in her constant companionship without finding it one of the greatest blessings of their lives."

"I think you must resemble her, auntie," said Evelyn with an affectionate, admiring look into Elsie's bright, sweet face."

"It is my desire to do so," she answered, flushing with pleasure. "My precious mother! I could hardly bear to leave her, Eva, even for your uncle's sake."

"But I am glad you did," quickly returned the little girl. "I am so glad to have you for my aunt."

"Thank you, dear," was the pleased rejoinder. "I have never regretted my choice or felt ashamed of having gone all the way to Italy to join my sick and suffering betrothed to become his wife that I might nurse him back to health."

"Oh, did you?" exclaimed Evelyn, looking full of interest and delight. "Please, tell me the whole story, won't you? I should so like to hear it."

Elsie willingly complied with the request, and it would be difficult to say who enjoyed the story most—she who told it or she who listened.

"I think you were brave and kind and good, Aunt Elsie," was Evelyn's comment when the tale was told.

"I had a strong motive—the saving of a life dearer to me than my own," Elsie responded, absently, as if her thoughts were busy with the past.

Both were silent for a little, Evelyn gazing with mournful eyes upon the lovely grounds and the beautiful scenery about her home.

"Aunt Elsie," she said at length, "do you know what is to be done with the house while mamma and I are away? If it should be left long unoccupied, it will fall into decay, and the grounds will become a wilderness of weeds."

"Your mother suggested having it rented just as it stands—ready furnished," replied Elsie. "But she feared—as do we also—that strangers might abuse the property. Then, as I thought it over, it occurred to me that we might rent it ourselves for a summer residence. When we are away from it, we can leave it in charge of Patrick and his wife, who have no children and who have lived so long in the family—

so your mother told us—that their character for trustworthiness is well established."

"Yes, indeed it is!" said Evelyn. "And that seems to me the best plan that could possibly be devised except that—"

"Well dear, except what?" Elsie asked pleasantly, as the little girl paused without finishing her sentence.

"I fear it will be a great expense to you and Uncle," was the half-hesitating reply. "And that you will get little good of it, being so far away nearly all the year."

"You are very thoughtful for one so young," said Elsie in surprise.

"It is because papa talked so much with me about his affairs and the uses of money—the difficulty of earning and keeping it and the best ways of economizing. He said he wanted to teach me how to take care of myself, if ever I were left alone in the world."

"That was wise and kind of your father," said Elsie. "I think you must have paid good attention to his teachings. But about the expense we shall incur in making the proposed arrangement—there is a large family of us, and I do not doubt that we shall have help with both the use of the house and the paying of the rent."

"Your mamma is very rich, I've heard," remarked Evelyn inquiringly.

"Very rich and very generous," returned her aunt.

"Are we to leave soon to go directly to your home?" asked Evelyn.

"It will be probably several weeks before your uncle can get everything arranged, and then he wants to spend some time sketching the scenery about Lake George and among the Adirondacks," replied Elsie. "And we are to go with him. Shall you like it, Eva?"

"Oh, yes, indeed!" Evelyn exclaimed, her face lighting up with pleasure. Then with gathering tears and in low, tremulous tones, she murmured, "Papa had promised to take me to both places someday," she said.

CHAPTER SEVENTH

Fairview and Ion

IT HAD BEEN A CLOUDY and overcast afternoon, and the rain began to fall as, shortly after sunset, the Lelands left the rail cars for the Fairview family carriage.

"A dismal homecoming for you, my love," remarked Lester, as the coachman closed the door on them and mounted to his perch again.

"Oh, no!" returned Elsie brightly. "The rain is needed, and we are well sheltered from it. Yet, I fear it may be dismal for Evelyn. But, my dear child, try to keep up your spirits. It does not always rain in this part of the country."

"Oh, no! Of course not, auntie," said the little girl with a low laugh of amusement. "I should not want to live here if it did not rain sometimes."

"I should think not, indeed," said her uncle. "Well, Eva, we will hope the warmth of your welcome will atone to you for the inclemency of the weather."

"Yes," said Elsie. "We want you to feel that it is a homecoming to you as well as to us."

"Thank you both very much," murmured Evelyn, her voice a little broken with the thought of her orphaned conditioned. "I shall try to be deserving of your great kindness."

"We have done nothing yet to call for so strong an expression of gratitude, Eva," remarked her uncle in a lively tone.

In the kitchen and dining room at Fairview great preparations were going forward. In the one a table was laid with the finest satin damask, glittering silver, cut glass, and china. In the other sounds and scents told of a coming, "feast of fat things."

"Clar to goodness! Ef it ain't a pourin' down like de clouds was a wantin' to drownd Miss Elsie an' de rest!" exclaimed a young girl, coming in from a back veranda, from whence she had been taking an observation of the weather. "An' it's that dark, Aunt Kitty, yo' couldn't see yo' hand afo' yo' face."

"Hope Uncle Cuff keep de road and don't upset the kerridge," returned Aunt Kitty, the cook, as she opened her oven door to glance at a fine, young fowl browning beautifully there and sending forth a most savory smell.

"He'd larf at every idear of upsettin' dat vehicle, he would, kase he tinks dar ain't nobody else knows de roads ekal to hisself. But den 'tain't always de folks what makes de biggest boastin' dat kin do de best, am it now, Lizzie?"

"No, I reckon 'tain't, Aunt Kitty, but doan you be prognosticatin' ob evil and skearin' folks out deir wits fo' de fac's am 'stablished."

"An' ain't gwine fo' to be 'stablished," put in another voice. "'Spose de family been trabling roun' de worl' to come back an' git harm right afo' deir own do'? 'Co'se not."

"Hark! Dere dey is dis bressed minit. I hear de soun' o' de wheels and de hosses' feet," exclaimed Aunt Kitty, slamming closed her oven door, laying down the spoon with which she had been basting her fowl, and hastily exchanging her dark, cotton apron for a white one.

She brought up the rear of the train of servants gathering in the hall to welcome their master and mistress home to Fairview.

A glad welcome it was, for both Lester and Elsie were greatly loved by their dependents. Evelyn, too, came in for a share of the hand shaking and the "God bless you's." She was assured again and again that she was most welcome at Fairview.

"Well, Aunt Kitty, I suppose you have one of your excellent suppers ready for us hungry travelers?" remarked Mr. Leland interrogatively as he divested himself of his duster.

"I'se done de wery bes' I knows, sah," she answered, dropping a curtsey and smiling all over her face. "Eberyting am done to a turn, an' I hopes you, sah, and de ladies mos' ready to eat afo' de tings get spoiled."

"We won't keep your supper waiting long, Aunt Kitty," said her mistress pleasantly.

"Myra, would you take the baby to the nursery? Evelyn, my dear, we will go upstairs and I will show you your room."

Reaching the second floor, Elsie led the way into a spacious, luxuriously furnished apartment.

"This is your room, Eva," she said. "It is just across the hall from your uncle's and mine, so I hope you will not feel lonely or timid. If anything should alarm you, come to our door and call us."

"Thank you, dear Aunt Elsie. Such a beautiful room it is!" exclaimed Evelyn. "How very kind you and Uncle Lester are to me!"

There was a little tremble of emotion in the child's voice as she spoke.

Elsie put her arms lovingly about her. "Dear child," she said, "how could we be otherwise? We want you to feel that this is truly your own home and to be very happy in it."

"I could not be so happy with anyone else as with you and uncle," returned the little girl with a sigh to the memory of the father she had loved so well.

"And tomorrow you shall see what a sweet home this is," Elsie said, releasing her with a kiss.

"Now, we must hasten to make ourselves ready for supper. A change of dress will not be necessary. There will be no company tonight, and your uncle would prefer seeing us in our traveling dresses to having his meal spoiled by waiting."

Evelyn went to sleep that night to the music of the dashing of the rain upon the windows, but she awoke the next morning to find the sun shining brightly in a deep, blue sky wherein soft, fleecy, white clouds were floating.

She drew aside the window curtain to take a peep at the surroundings of her new home. Lawn, shrubbery, flower garden, while larger than those at Crag Cottage, were quite as well kept. Neatness and order, beauty and fragrance made them so attractive that Evelyn was tempted to a stroll while waiting for the call to breakfast.

She stole softly down the stairs, thinking her aunt and uncle might be still sleeping, but instead she found the latter on the veranda pacing to and fro with a meditative air.

"Ah, good morning, my little maid!" he said in a very kindly tone. "I certainly hope to hear that my niece slept well and feels quite refreshed on this beautiful morning?"

"Yes, uncle, thank you," she returned. "Don't you enjoy being at home again after your long absence?"

"I do indeed!" he answered. "There is no place like home, is there? This is your home, too, now, Eva."

"Yes, sir," she said a little sadly. "You and Aunt Elsie are home to me now, almost as papa used to be in the dear old days. Perhaps I shall learn to love Fairview as well as I do Crag Cottage. May I go into the garden, uncle?"

"Yes, I will take you with pleasure. Your shoes are thick, I see," he observed, glancing down at them. "That is well, for the early morning walks may be a little damp."

He led her about, calling her attention to one and another rare plant or flower in the garden and greenhouse. Then he gathered a bouquet of beautiful and fragrant blossoms for her and then one for his wife.

Elsie joined them on the veranda as they came in at the summons to breakfast, and Lester presented his flowers, claiming a kiss in return.

"Help yourself," she said laughingly. "Many thanks for your flowers. Now, shall we go in to breakfast? We are a little late this morning."

"Ah, the mail is already here this morning, I see," Lester remarked, as they entered the breakfast room. "I will open the bag while you pour the coffee, my dear, hoping to find a letter for each of us."

"I think there should be one for me," remarked Evelyn, watching her uncle with wistful, longing eyes as he took out the letters and glanced over the addresses. "For I have heard but once from mamma since she went away."

"Twice now," her uncle said with a pleased smile, as he handed her the longed-for missive.

"You, too, hear from your mother this morning, my dear, and from several other friends. Here, Jane," to the servant girl in waiting. "Hand these to your mistress, please."

"And here is a cup of coffee to reward you— mamma's letter alone is worth it," responded Elsie brightly, lifting the letters from the silver tray on which they lay and setting there, in their stead, a delicate china cup from whose steaming contents a delicious aroma greeted the nostrils.

"I must peep into mamma's to see when we may expect them home," she added, breaking open its envelope. "The rest will keep till after breakfast."

"When was Aunt Wealthy's birthday?" queried her husband.

"Yesterday," she answered with her eyes on the letter. "Ah, Ned and Zoe start this morning for home. The rest will stay a week or so longer. Our cousins, Mr. and Mrs. Keith, and their daughter, Annis, will soon follow with the expectation of spending the winter as mamma's guests."

"Will you excuse me, Aunt Elsie, if I open my letter now for just a peep?" asked Evelyn with a slightly shy smile.

"No, my dear, certainly not. As I never do the like myself but always wait patiently till the meal is over," returned the young aunt with playful irony.

"Then I'll have to ask uncle or do it without permission," said Evelyn, blushing and laughing.

"Hark to the answer coming from the chicken yard," said her uncle facetiously, as the loud crow of a cock broke in upon their talk.

"I fail to catch your meaning, uncle," said Evelyn with another blush and smile.

"Listen!" he answered. "He will speak again presently, and tell me if he doesn't say, 'Mistress rules here.' Someone has so interpreted it and, I think, correctly."

"Oh!" exclaimed Evelyn, laughing. "Then, of course, it is of no use to appeal from auntie's decisions."

"No, even I generally do as I am bid," he remarked gravely.

"And I almost always," said Elsie. "Eva, would you like to drive over to Ion with me this morning?"

"Very much indeed, Aunt Elsie," was the prompt and pleased reply.

"Mamma wishes me to carry the news of the expected arrival of my brother and his wife and to see that all is in order for their reception," Elsie went on.

"Am I to be entirely neglected in your invitation?" asked her husband in a tone of deep pretended disappointment and chagrin.

"Your company will be most acceptable, Mr. Leland, if you will favor us with it," was the happy rejoinder. "Baby shall go, too. An airing will do him good. And besides, mammy will want to see him."

"Of course, for she looks upon him as a sort of great-grandchild, does she not?" said Lester.

"Either that or great-great," returned Elsie lightly.

"Who is mammy?" asked Evelyn.

"Mamma's old nurse, who had the care of her from birth—and of her mother also—and has nursed each one of us in turn. Of course, we are all devotedly attached to her and she to us. Aunt Chloe is what she is called by those who are not her nurslings."

"She must be very, very old, I should think," observed Evelyn.

"She is," said Elsie, "and very infirm. No one knows her exact age, but she cannot be much younger than Aunt Wealthy, who has just passed her hundredth birthday. I actually believe her to be somewhat older."

"How I should like to see her!" exclaimed Evelyn.

"I hope to give you that pleasure today," responded Elsie. "Until very recently she always accompanied mamma—no, I am mistaken—she stayed behind once. It was when Lily was taken North as a last hope of saving her dear life. Papa and mamma thought it best to take me and the baby along and to leave mammy behind in charge of the other children.

"This summer she was too feeble to leave Ion, so we shall find her there. In deep sorrow, too, no doubt. Her old husband, Uncle Joe, died a few weeks ago."

"Eva must hear their story one of these days," remarked Mr. Leland. "It is very interesting."

"Yes, and some of it is very sad—that which occurred before mamma's visit to Viamede after she had reached her majority. That visit was the dawn of brighter days to them. I will tell you the whole story, Eva, some time when we are sitting quietly together at our needlework, if you will remind me."

"For what hour will you have the carriage ordered, my dear?" Lester asked as they left the breakfast table.

"Ten, if you please," she answered. "I hope you will go with us?"

"I shall do so with pleasure," he said. "It is a lovely morning for a drive. The rain has laid the dust, and the air is just cool enough to be bracing."

Evelyn was on the veranda, gazing about her with a thoughtful air.

"Well, lassie, what think you of Fairview?" asked her uncle, coming to her side.

"I like it," she answered emphatically. "Didn't something happen here, uncle, in the time of the Klu Klux raids? I seem to have heard there did."

"Yes, a coffin with a threatening notice attached was laid at the gate yonder one night. My uncle owned and lived on the place at that time, and by reason of his northern birth and Republican sentiments, was odious to the members of the Klan."

"And it was he they were threatening?"

"Yes. They afterward attacked the place, wounded and drove him into the woods, but they were held at bay and finally driven off by the gallant defense of her home by my aunt. She was assisted by her son, who was then quite a young boy.

"But get Elsie to tell you the story. She can do it far better than I—especially as she was living at Ion at that time. Though a mere child, she has still a vivid recollection of all the circumstances."

"Yes," Elsie said, "including the attacks upon Ion—first the quarter, when they burned the schoolhouse, and afterward the mansion. There were several sad scenes connected with them."

"How interesting to hear all about them from an eye witness," exclaimed Evelyn. "I am eager to have you begin, Aunt Elsie."

"Perhaps I may be able to do so this evening," returned her aunt. "But now I must give my orders for the day about the house and then it will almost be time for our drive."

"What does your mamma say?" asked Lester of Evelyn when Elsie left them alone together.

"Not very much that I care for uncle," sighed the little girl. "She's in good health, but she already tires of foreign cookery—wishes she could have such a breakfast every morning as she has been accustomed to at home. Still, she enjoys the sights and thinks it may be a year, or longer, before she gets backs. She describes some of the places and paintings and statuary she has seen, but that part of the letter I have not read yet."

"Do you wish you were with her, Eva?" he asked, smoothing her hair as she stood by his side, gazing affectionately at her.

"No, uncle, I should like to see mamma, of course, but at present I like this quiet home far better than going about among crowds of strange people."

He looked pleased. "I am glad you are content," he said.

Elsie was full of life and merriment as they set out upon their drive. Her husband remarked on it with great pleasure.

"Yes," she said lightly. "It is nice to be going back to my old, childhood home after so long an absence—to see mammy, too—dear old mammy! And yet it will hardly seem like home either, without mamma there."

"No," he responded. "But it is quite delightful to look forward to having her there in her rightful place again in a week or two."

They had turned in at the great gates leading into the avenue, and presently Elsie, glancing eagerly toward the house, exclaimed with delight, "Ah, there is mammy on the veranda! She's watching for our coming, no doubt. She knew we were expected at Fairview yesterday, and that I would not be long in finding my way to Ion."

Evelyn, looking out also, perceived a bent and shriveled form seated in an armchair, leaning forward. The two dusky hands clasped a stout cane and her chin rested on the top.

As the carriage drew up before the entrance, the figure rose slowly and stiffly, and with the aid of the cane, she hobbled across the veranda to meet them.

"Bress de Lawd!" she cried in accents tremulous with age and excitement. "It's one ob my chillens, sho' nuff. It's Miss Elsie!"

"Yes, mammy, it is I, and very glad I am to see you," responded Mrs. Leland, hurrying up the veranda steps and throwing her arms about the feeble, trembling form.

"Poor old mammy," she said tenderly. "You are not so strong as you used to be."

"No, darlin', yo' ole mammy's mos' at de brink ob de ribber. De cold watahs ob Jordan soon be creepin' up roun' her ole feet."

"But you are not afraid, my dear mammy?" Elsie said, tears trembling in the sweet, soft eyes so like her mother's.

"No, chile, no—for Ise got fas' hold ob de Master's hand, and He holds me tight. De waves can't go ober my head, kase He bought me wid His own precious blood and I b'longs to Him, and He always takes care ob His own chillens."

"Yes, Aunt Chloe," Lester said, taking one of her withered hands in his. Elsie withdrew from her embrace and turned aside to wipe away a tear. "His purchased ones are safe for time and for eternity."

"'The Lord God is a sun and shield; the Lord will give grace and glory.'"

"Dat's so, sah, grace to lib by, an' grace to die by, den glory wid Him in heaben! Ole Uncle Joe done 'speriencin' dat now—an' bymeby dis chile be wid him dar."

"And who dis?" she asked, catching sight of Evelyn standing by her side and regarding her with tearful eyes.

"My niece, Evelyn Leland, Aunt Chloe," answered Lester. "She has heard all about you and wanted to meet you."

"God bress you, honey," Chloe said, taking the little girl's hand in hers and regarding her with a look of kindly interest.

The other servants had come flocking to the veranda as the news of the arrival passed from lip to lip. And now they crowded about Lester and Elsie eager to shake their hands and bid them welcome home again. Mingled with their rejoicings and congratulations came many inquiries about their loved mistress—her mother—and the other absent members of the family.

And here, as at Fairview, Evelyn received her full share of pleased attention.

Elsie delivered her mother's messages and household directions, and taking Evelyn with her, she went through the house to see that all was in order for the reception of her brother and his wife. They then sat down on the veranda for a chat with "mammy" before returning to Fairview.

"Mammy, dear," she said interrogatively, "you are not grieving very much for Uncle Joe?"

"No, chile, no. He's in dat bressed land whar dah no mo' misery in de back, in de head, in any part ob de body. An' dere ain't no mo' sin, no mo' sorrow, no mo' dying, no mo' tears fallin' down the cheeks, no mo' trouble any kin'."

"But don't you miss him very much, Aunt Chloe?" asked Evelyn softly, her voice tremulous with the thought of her own beloved dead and how sorely she felt his absence.

"Yes, chile, sho I does, but 'twon't be for long. Ise so ole and weak dat I knows Ise mos' dar. Ise mos' dar!"

The black, wrinkled face uplifted to the sky almost shone with glad expectancy, and the dim, sunken eyes grew bright for an instant with hope and joy.

Then turning them upon Evelyn, and, for the first time, she noticed her deep mourning. "Po' chile," she said in tender pitying tones. "Yo's loss somebody dat yo' near kin?"

Evelyn nodded, her heart too full for speech, and Elsie said softly, "Her dear father has gone to be forever with the Lord in the blessed, happy land you have been speaking of, mammy."

"Bressed, happy man!" exclaimed the aged saint, again lifting her head heavenward. "An' bressed happy chile dat has de great an' mighty God for her father—kase de good book say He is the father of de fatherless."

A momentary hush fell upon the little group. Then Mr. Leland, who had been looking into the condition of the field and garden, as his wife into that of the house, joined them and suggested that this would be a good time and place for the telling of the story Eva had been asking for, especially as, in Aunt Chloe, they had a second eye witness.

Elsie explained to her what was wanted.

"Ah, chillens, dat was a terrible time," returned the old woman, sighing and shaking her head.

"Yes, mammy," assented Elsie. "You remember it well, don't you?"

"'Deed I does, chile." Rousing now with the recollection into almost youthful excitement and energy, she plunged into the story, telling it in a graphic way that enraptured her listeners— though to two of them it was not new, and one occasionally assisted her memory or supplied a missing link in the chain of circumstances.

CHAPTER EIGHTH

Next stood hypocrisy, with holy leer,
Soft smiling and demurely looking down,
But hid the dagger underneath the gown.

—*Dryden*

WHILE OLD MAMMY told her story to her three listeners on the veranda at Ion, a train was speeding southward, bearing Edward and Zoe on their homeward way.

Zoe, in charmingly elegant traveling attire with her fond young husband by her side ready to anticipate every wish and gratify it if in his power, was extremely comfortable. She found great enjoyment—now in chatting merrily with him, now sitting silent by his side watching the flying panorama of forest and prairie, hill, valley, rock, river, and plain.

At length, however, her attention was attracted to something going on within the car.

"Tickets!" cried the conductor, passing down the aisle. "Tickets!"

Edward handed out his own and his wife's. They were duly punched and given back.

The conductor moved on his way, repeating his call, "Tickets?"

Up to this moment Zoe had scarcely noticed who occupied the seat immediately behind herself and Edward, but now turning her head, she saw there two young women of pleasing appearance, evidently foreigners. Both were looking anxiously up at the conductor who held their tickets in his hand.

"You are on the wrong road," he was saying. "These are through-tickets for Utah."

"What does he say? Something is wrong?" asked the younger of the two girls, addressing her companion in Danish.

"I do not understand, Alma," replied the other, speaking in the same tongue. "Ah, did we but know English! I do not understand, sir. I do not know one word you say," she repeated with a hopeless shake of the head, addressing the conductor.

"Do you know what she says, sir?" asked the man, turning to Edward.

"From her looks and gestures it is evident that she does not understand English," replied Edward. "And I think that is what she says. Suppose you try her with German."

"Can't, sir. I speak no language but my mother tongue. Perhaps you will do me the favor and act as an interpreter?"

"With pleasure," he replied. Addressing the young woman, Edward asked in German if she spoke that language.

She answered with an eager affirmative, and he went on to explain that the ticket she had offered the conductor would not pay her fare on that road. Then he asked where she wished to go.

"To Utah, sir," she said. "Is not this the road to take us there?"

"No, we are traveling south, and Utah lies toward the northwest — very far west."

"Oh, sir, what shall we do?" she exclaimed in great distress. "Will they stop the cars and let us out?"

"Not just here. The conductor says you can get off at the next station and wait there for a train going back to Cincinnati. It seems it must have been there you made the mistake and left your proper route, and there you can recover it."

She sat silent, looking sadly bewildered and also greatly distressed.

"I feel sorry for you," said Zoe kindly, speaking in German. "We would be glad to help you, and if you like to tell us your story, my husband may be able to advise you what to do."

"I am sure you are kind and good, dear lady — both you and the gentleman, and I will gladly tell you all," was the reply after a moment's hesitation. In a few rapid sentences she explained that she and Alma, her younger sister, had been orphaned and destitute in Norway, their native land, and after a hard struggle of several months had fallen in with a Mormon missionary who gave them glowing accounts of Utah, telling them it was the paradise of the poor. He promised that if they would go with him and become members of the Mormon Church, land would be given them, their poverty and hard toil would become a thing of the past, and they would live in blissful enjoyment among the Latter-day Saints — where rich and poor were treated alike, as neighbors and friends.

She said that at first they could scarcely endure the thought of leaving their dear, native land, but so bright was the picture drawn by the Mormon, that at length they decided to go with him.

They gathered up their few possessions, bade a tearful farewell to old neighbors and friends, and set sail for America in the company of two or three hundred other Mormon converts.

Their expectation was to travel all the way to Salt Lake City in the company, but, as they neared the end of the voyage, Alma fell ill. When they landed she was so entirely unfit for travel that they were compelled to remain behind for several weeks at an expense that so rapidly diminished their small store of money that when, at last, they set out on their long journey across the country, they were almost literally penniless.

They had, however, the through-ticket to Utah—which the Mormon missionary had made them buy before leaving them. Knowing no choice and believing all his wily misrepresentations, they rejoiced in its possession as the passport to an earthly paradise.

"But we have lost our way," concluded Christine with a look of distress. "How are we to find it? How can we make sure of not again straying from the right path? Kind sir, can you, will you, give us some advice? Could I in any way earn the money to pay for our travel on this road? I know how to work and I am strong and willing."

Edward mused a moment, then said, "We will consider that question presently, but let us first have a little more talk.

"Ah, what can be the matter?" he exclaimed in English, starting up to glance from the window. The train had come to a sudden standstill in a bit of woods where there seemed no occasion for stopping. "What is wrong?" he asked of a man hurrying by toward the engine.

"A wreck ahead, sir," was the reply.

Every man in the car had risen from his seat and was hastening to alight and view the scene of the disaster that lay ahead.

"Oh, Ned, is there any danger?" asked Zoe.

"No, dear, I think not. You won't mind if I leave you for a moment to learn how long we are likely to be detained here?"

"No, I won't, if you promise to be careful not to get into danger," she said with some hesitation. He hurried after the others.

Alma and Christine, looking pale and anxious, asked Zoe what was the matter.

She explained that there had been an accident—collision of cars—and that the broken fragments were lying on the track and would have to be cleared away before their train could go on.

Then Edward came back with the news that there would be a delay of an hour or more.

Zoe uttered a slight exclamation of impatience.

"Let us not grumble, little wife," he said cheerily. "We should be thankful that things are no worse. And, do you know, I trust it will prove to have been a good providence, inasmuch as it gives us an opportunity to make an effort to rescue these poor dupes from the Mormon net."

"Oh, yes," she said, her countenance brightening. "I do hope so! Let us try to convince them not to go to Utah."

"I shall do my best," he said. Then, addressing Christine again—in German as before, "Will you tell me what are the teachings of Mormonism, according to your missionary?"

"They believe the Bible," she answered. "They preach the gospel of Christ as the Bible teaches it, else how could I have listened to him? How could I have consented to go with him? I know the Bible is God's Word, and that there can be no salvation out of Christ."

"Did he not tell you that they teach and practice polygamy, ma'am?"

"No, sir, no indeed! It surely cannot be true?"

"I am sorry to say it is only too true," said Edward. "The Mormon priesthood do both teach and practice it. One of them, Orson Pratt, in a sermon preached August 29, 1852, said: 'The Latter-day Saints have embraced the doctrine of a plurality of wives as a part of their religious faith. It is incorporated as a part of our religion, and necessary for our exaltation to the fullness of the Lord's glory in the eternal world.'"

Christine looked inexpressibly shocked. "Oh, sir, are you quite sure of it?" she cried. "Not a word of such a doctrine was spoken to us. Had it been we would never have set out for Utah."

"It is a well-established fact," replied Edward. "It is well known also that they conceal this doctrine from those whom they wish to catch in their net. To them they exalt the Bible and Christ. But when the poor dupes reach their promised paradise and are unable to escape, they find the Bible kicked into a corner, the book of Mormon substituted for it, and Joe Smith exalted above the Lord Jesus Christ."

"Dreadful!" exclaimed Christine.

Alma, too, looked greatly shocked.

"But women may remain single if they choose?" she said inquiringly.

"No, indeed!" replied Edward. "The Mormon theology teaches that those who are faithful Mormons, living up to their privileges and having a plurality of wives, will be kings in the celestial world, and their wives queens. While those who have but one wife—though they will reach heaven if they are faithful to the priesthood and in paying tithes—will not have a place of honor there. And those who are not married at all will be slaves to the polygamists.

"For this reason, they desire to have many wives. And they will have them, willing or unwilling.

"They send their missionaries abroad to recruit the Mormon ranks and supply wives for those who want them.

"The missionaries procure photographs of the single women whom they have persuaded to embrace Mormonism, and these are sent on in advance of the parties of emigrants. The Mormon men who want wives are then invited to look at the photographs and select for themselves.

"They do so, and when the train comes in bringing the originals of the pictures, they are there to meet it. Each man seizes the girl he has chosen by photograph and drags her away—often shrieking for help, which no one gives. I have this on the testimony of the minister of the Presbyterian Church who has lived for years in Utah."

Alma grasped her sister's arm, her cheek paling, her eyes wild with fright.

"Oh, Christine! You know as well as I do that he has our likenesses. You know we gave them to him, as he asked, suspecting no harm. Oh, what shall we do?"

"Be calm, sister. God has preserved us from that dreadful fate," said Christine with quivering lips. "I know not what is to become of us, penniless in a strange land, but we will never go there—no, not if we starve to death."

"You need not do that," exclaimed Zoe. "No one who is willing to work need starve in this good land. My husband and I will befriend you and help you find employment."

"Oh, many thanks, dear lady!" cried the sisters in a breath. "It is all we ask. We are ready, able, and willing to work."

"What can you do?" asked Edward. "What were you expecting to do in Utah?"

"We were to have some land," said Christine. "That was the promise, and we thought to raise vegetables and fruits, fowls, too, and perhaps bees. But we can cook, wash the clothes, keep the house, clean, spin, weave, and sew."

"Oh," said Zoe, "if you know how to do all those things—well, there will be no trouble in finding employment for you."

"But where, dear lady?" Christine asked with hesitation. "We have no money to pay our way to travel far. We must find work near at hand, or not at all."

Zoe gave her husband a look, inquiring and entreating, but he seemed lost in thought and did not see it.

He was anxious to help these poor strangers, but without wounding the pride of their independence, which he perceived and also respected. Presently he spoke. "My wife and I live at some distance from here. We are not acquainted in this vicinity, but we know there is plenty of such work as you want in our own. If you like, I will advance your traveling expenses and engage to find employment for you. You can repay the advance when it suits you."

The generous offer was immediately accepted with deep gratitude.

The delay of their train lasted some time longer, and presently talk about Mormonism was renewed.

It was Alma who began it by asking if a Mormon's first wife was always willing that he should take a second.

"Oh, no, no!" Zoe exclaimed. "How could she be?"

"No," said Edward. "But she is considered very wicked if she refuses her consent or even ventures upon a remonstrance.

"One day a Mormon and his family, consisting of one wife and several children, were seated about their table taking a meal, when the husband remarked that he thought of taking a second wife.

"His lawful wife—the mother of his children sitting there—objected. Upon that he rose from his seat, went to her, and, holding her head, deliberately cut her throat from ear to ear."

"And was he executed for it?" asked Christine while she shuddered with horror.

"No," said Edward. "He was promoted by the Mormon priesthood to a higher place in the church, as one who had done a praiseworthy deed."

"Murder a praiseworthy deed!" they cried in astonishment and indignation. "How could that be so?"

"They have a doctrine that they call 'blood atonement,'" replied Edward. "Daring to teach, contrary to the express declarations of Scripture, that the blood of Christ is insufficient to atone for all sin, they assert that for some sins the blood of the sinner himself must be shed or he will never attain to eternal life, and that, therefore, it is a worthy deed to slay him.

"That terrible, wicked doctrine has been made the excuse for many assassinations. It was the ground for not only excusing the horrible crime of which I have just told you, but for also rewarding the wretched criminal.

"Polygamy is bad enough—especially as instances are not wanting of a man being married at the same time to a mother and her daughters, or several sisters, and in at least one instance to mother, daughter, and granddaughter. Mormon theology teaches, too, that a man may lawfully marry his own sister. Yet it is not the worst of their crimes. We have it upon the testimony of credible witnesses—Christian citizens of Salt Lake City—that their temples and tithing-houses are 'built up by extortion and cemented with the blood of men, women, and children whose only offense was that they were not in sympathy with the unrighteous decrees of this usurping priesthood.' And 'that all manner of social abominations and domestic horrors and mutilations, blood atonings, assassinations, and massacres have been perpetrated in the name and by the authority of the Mormon priesthood.'"

"Oh, sir, how very, very dreadful!" exclaimed Christine. "Are they not afraid of the judgments of God against such fearfully wicked deeds?"

"It seems not. The Bible speaks of some whose consciences are seared as with a hot iron," he said.

"But why is such terrible wickedness and awful oppression allowed by your government?"

"There you have asked a question that many of our own people are asking. It is difficult to answer without bringing a heavy charge against our law makers at Washington—a charge of gross neglect—whether induced by bribery or not I do not pretend to decide."

"But what makes us blush for the honor of the land we love!" cried Zoe with heightened color and flashing eyes.

CHAPTER NINTH

Heaven gives us friends.

THE TRAIN MOVED ON and Zoe settled herself back in her seat with a contented sigh. It was nice to think of soon being home again after months of absence. She had grown to love Ion very much, and she was charmed with the idea of being mistress of the household for the week or two that was to elapse before the return of the rest of the family.

But she was greatly interested in the Norwegian girls and presently began to occupy herself with plans for their benefit.

Edward watched her furtively, quite amused at the unwonted gravity of her countenance.

"What, may I ask, is the subject of your serious meditations, little woman?" he inquired with a laughing look into her face, as the train came to a momentary standstill at a country station. "One might suppose, from your exceeding grave and pre-occupied air, that you were engaged in settling the affairs of the nation."

"No, no, my load of care is somewhat lighter than that, Mr. Travilla," she returned with mock seriousness. "It is those poor girls I am thinking of and of what employment can be found for them."

"Well, what is the conclusion arrived at? Or is there none as yet?"

"I think—I am nearly sure, indeed—that if they are really expert needlewomen, we can find plenty for them to do in our own family connection—five families of us, you know."

"Five?"

"Yes, Ion, Fairview, The Laurels, The Oaks, and Roselands, too."

"Ah, yes, and it must take an immense amount of sewing to provide all the changes of raiment desired by the ladies and children," he remarked laughingly. "So that matter may be considered arranged and my little wife freed from care."

"No, I have yet to consider how they are to be conveyed from the city to Ion and what I am to do with them when I get them there. Mamma will not be there to direct, you know."

"The first question is easily settled. I shall hire a hack for their use. As to the other, why not let them have their meals served in the sewing room and occupy the bedroom opening into it?"

"Why, to be sure! That will do nicely," she said. "If you think mamma would not object."

"I am quite certain she will find no fault, even if she should make a different arrangement on returning home. And you wouldn't mind that, would you, my dear?"

"Oh, no, indeed! Are we not going very fast?"

"Yes, trying to make up lost time."

"I hope they will succeed so that our supper may not be spoiled with waiting. Do you think there will be anyone but the servants at Ion to watch for our coming, Ned?"

"Yes, I expect to find the Fairview family there and have some hope of seeing delegations from the other three. Mamma wrote Elsie when to look for us, and probably she has let the others know. All of them who have been absent from home this summer returned some days or weeks ago."

"And Lester and Elsie brought that orphan niece of his home with them, I suppose. I am inclined to be a warm friend to her, Ned, for I know how to feel for a fatherless child."

"As we all do, I trust. We are all fatherless and may well have a fellow-feeling for her. We will do what we can to make life pleasant to her, and I think from my sister's report that we shall find her an agreeable addition to the Fairview family."

Elsie had given to Evelyn quite as agreeable a portraiture of Edward and Zoe as that she had furnished them of her, and the little girl was in some haste to make their acquaintance.

It was as Edward expected. The five families were very sociable. When all were at home there was a constant interchange of informal visits, and when some of their number returned after a lengthened absence, the others were ready to hail their coming with cordiality and delight—both of which were intensified on this occasion by the relief from the fear that some accident had happened to Edward and Zoe, inasmuch as they were several hours behind time in reaching home.

Their arrival found the Lelands, the Lacys, the Dinsmores, and the Conlys gathered in the drawing room and supper waiting.

"Two hours behind time! I really am afraid there has been an accident," Mrs. Lacy was saying when the welcome sound of wheels called forth a general exclamation. "There they are at last!" There was a simultaneous exit from the drawing room into the hall followed by numerous embraces, welcomes, congratulations, inquiries after health, and the cause of the delay.

They made a jovial party about the supper table—all but Evelyn, who sat silently listening to the exchange of information in regard to the way in which each had passed the summer and Edward and Zoe's description of the celebration of their Aunt Wealthy's one hundredth birthday. All was mingled with jest, laughter, and merry banter.

As the child looked and listened she was, quite unconsciously, studying countenances, voices, words, and forming estimates of character.

She had been doing so all evening. She had already decided that the Lacys and Dinsmores were nice people who made her feel happy and at home with them. She also liked Mr. Calhoun Conly and his brother Dr. Arthur very much, but she detested Ralph, thought Ella silly, proud, and haughty—and that with no excuse for either pride or arrogance. So now her principal attention was given to the latest arrivals—Edward and Zoe.

She liked them both—thinking it lovely to see their devotion to each other and how unconsciously it betrayed itself in looks and tones, now and again, as the talk went on.

At length, as the flow of conversation slacked, Zoe turned to Evelyn, remarking with a winning smile, "What a quiet little mouse you are! I have been wanting to make your acquaintance, and I hope you will come often to Ion."

"Thank you. I shall enjoy doing so very much indeed," returned Evelyn, blushing with pleasure. Edward seconded the invitation.

"And don't forget that the doors are wide open to you at the Laurels," said Mr. Lacy.

"At the Oaks also," said Mr. Dinsmore. And Calhoun Conly added, "At Roselands we shall expect frequent visits and do our best for your entertainment, though unfortunately we have no little folks to be your companions."

Evelyn acknowledged each invitation gracefully and in suitable words. Then, the meal having come to a conclusion, all rose from the table and returned to the drawing room. Presently, as it was growing late and the travelers were supposed to be wearied with their journey, one family after another bade good-bye and departed.

"Well, Eva, what do you think of Mrs. Zoe?" asked Mr. Leland when they had turned out of the avenue into the road leading to Fairview. "It was my understanding you were quite anxious to make her acquaintance."

"I think I shall like her very much, uncle," Eva answered. "She seems so bright, pleasant, and cordial. And she loves her husband so dearly."

Mr. Leland laughed at the concluding words. "And you think that is an additional reason for liking her?"

"Yes, indeed! I think husbands and wives should be very unselfishly affectionate toward each other as I have observed that you and Aunt Elsie always are with each other."

Both laughed in a pleased way, her uncle saying, "So you have been watching us?"

"I never set myself at it," she said. "But I couldn't help seeing what was so evident."

"And no harm if you did. Eva, not to change the subject, but I am greatly interested in those Norwegians. I hope, my dear, that you can give them some employment from Fairview."

"Yes, and I shall do so gladly if they are competent as claimed—for I feel a deep interest in them."

"So do I," said Evelyn. "I wanted to meet them."

"We will call at Ion again tomorrow, and I think you will then get a sight of them. I will learn then something of their ability in the sewing line," said her aunt.

Edward and Zoe had arrived at home a little in advance of their two proteges and had given orders in regard to their reception. When the girls reached Ion, they were received by Aunt Dicey, the house-keeper, kindly welcomed, and conducted to the apartments assigned them, where they found a tempting meal spread for their refreshment and every comfort provided.

"Dis am de sewin' room—an' fo' de present yo' dinin' room also," she announced as she ushered them in. "An' dat am de bedroom whar Mr. Ed'ard an' Miss Zoe tole me you uns is to sleep. Dar's watah dar an' soap an' towels, s'posin' you likes fo' to wash off de dust ob trabel befo' you sits down to de table. 'Bout de time you gits done dat de hot cakes and toast and tea'll be fotched up from de kitchen."

With that she turned and left the room.

They stood for a moment gazing in a bewildered way each into the other's face. Not one word had they understood, but the gestures had been more intelligible. Aunt Dicey had pointed toward the open door of the adjoining room, and they comprehended that it was intended for their occupancy.

"What a dark-skinned woman, sister," said Alma at last. "What did she say? What language was that she was speaking?"

Christine shook her head. "Could it be English? I do not know. It did not sound like the English the gentleman and lady spoke when talking to each other. But she brought us here, and from the motions she made while talking, I think she said these two rooms were for us to use."

"These rooms for us? These beautiful rooms?" exclaimed Alma in astonishment and delight, glancing about upon the neat, tasteful, even elegant appointments of the one in which they were. Then hastening into the other, she found it in no way inferior to the first. "Ah, how lovely!" she cried. "See the pretty furniture, the white curtains trimmed with lace, the bed all white and looking, oh, so comfortable! Everything's so clean, so fair and sweet!"

"Yes, yes," said Christine, tears trembling in her eyes. "So far better than we ever dreamed. But it may be only for tonight—tomorrow, perhaps we may be consigned to lodgings not half so good. Ah, I hear steps on the stairs. They will be bringing our supper. Let us wash the dust from hands and face that we may be ready to eat."

Presently, seated at the table, they found an abundant appetite for the food set before them and remarked to each other again and again how very delicious it was—the best they had tasted in many, many days.

"We have fallen in with the best of friends, Christine," said Alma. "Have we not, sister? Oh, what a fortunate mistake was that that put us on the wrong road!"

"It was by the good guidance of our God, Alma," said Christine. "And, oh, how shortsighted and mistaken were we in mourning as we did over the sickness that separated us from the rest of our company and left us to travel alone in a strange land—alone and penniless!"

"We will have more faith in the future," said Alma. "We will trust the Lord, even when all is dark, and we cannot see one step before us."

"God helping us," added Christine devoutly. "But alas, we are prone to unbelief. When all is bright and the path lies straight before us, we feel strong in faith. When clouds and darkness cover it from sight, our faith is apt to fail, and our hearts to faint within us."

When the last of their guests of the evening had gone, Edward and Zoe sought out their proteges, going to the sewing room to inquire how they were and if they had been provided with everything necessary to their comfort.

They found Christine seated in an armchair by the table with the lamp drawn near her and reading from a pocket Testament. She closed and laid it aside on their entrance, rising to give them a respectful greeting.

"Where is your sister?" asked Zoe, glancing around the room in search of Alma.

Christine explained that, not having entirely recovered her strength since her illness, Alma was much fatigued with their journey and had already retired to rest.

"Quite right," said Edward. "I think you should follow her example very soon—for you, too, are looking tired. I hope the servants have attended to all your wants?"

"Oh, sir, and dear lady!" she exclaimed. "How good, how kind you are to us! What more could we possibly ask than has already been provided us by your orders?"

"Our orders were that you should be well cared for," Edward said. "But we feared that for lack of an interpreter you might not be able to make your wants known."

"Indeed, sir, every want was anticipated," she answered with grateful look and tone.

"That is well," he responded. "And now we will leave you to take your rest. Good night."

"Good night, sir," she said. Then, turning to Zoe, "And you, dear lady, will let me do some work for you tomorrow?"

"Yes, if you are quite rested by that time," was the smiling reply. "Don't be uneasy. Work and good wages will be found in abundance if you prove yourself capable."

So Christine went to bed with a heart singing for joy and thankfulness.

Elsie and Evelyn drove over to Ion next morning and found Zoe attending to her housekeeping cares with a pretty, matronly air that became her well. Aunt Dicey was receiving her orders with the look and manner of one who was humoring a child—for such she considered the youthful lady.

"There, Aunt Dicey, I believe that is all for today," said Zoe. Turning from Aunt Dicey to her callers, she cried, "Sister Elsie, how good of you to come over so early! And you, too, little maid," to Evelyn. "I'm delighted to see you both."

"Thank you," returned Elsie, brightly. "How do you like housekeeping?"

"Very much so far, and my efforts seem to amuse Ned immensely," laughed Zoe. "It's too absurd that he will persist in looking upon me still as a mere child. Just think of it! I've been married more than a year. Yes, a year and a half now."

"Ah, my dear little sister, don't be in too great a hurry to grow old," said Elsie. "Or you may be wanting to turn about and travel back again one of these days. How do you like your new helpers, or rather, their work? But I suppose you have hardly tried them yet."

"Yes, they are busy now in the sewing room. I wanted them to take a few days to rest, but their pride of independence rose up so against it that I was fairly forced to give them something to do. I was happy to find they do sew beautifully. Suppose you come and examine their work for yourself. You are included in the invitation, Evelyn," she added as she rose and led the way.

In the cheerful, sunny sewing room beside a window that looked out upon the beautiful grounds now bright with autumn flowers, Christine and Alma sat busily plying their needles. They were talking together thankfully of the present and hopefully of the future when the door opened and the two ladies and the little girl entered.

"How very industrious you two are!" said Zoe. "I have brought my sister, Mrs. Leland, to see what competent needlewomen you are."

"They are that indeed," Elsie said, examining the work. "I shall be glad to engage you both to sew for me when you are no longer needed here," she added with a kindly glance and smile.

Elsie took the chair that Zoe had drawn forward for her, and she entered into conversation with the strangers, asking of their past history and their plans, hopes, and wishes for the future—completely winning their confidence by her sweetly sympathizing tones and manner.

They were delighted with her, and she much pleased with them. Christine had a good, strong face and plain, rugged features, but a countenance that indicated so much good sense, honesty, and kindliness of heart that it was attractive in spite of its lack of comeliness.

Alma seemed to lean very much upon this older sister. Hers was a more delicate organization. She was timid and shrinking. With her fair complexion, deep blue eyes, golden hair, and look of refinement, she was really quite pretty and very ladylike in appearance.

CHAPTER TENTH

Who knows the joys of friendship—
The trust, security, and mutual tenderness,
The double joys, where each is glad for both?

— *R*OWE

MAX RAYMOND WAS racing about Miss Stanhope's grounds with the dog that had given his sister Lulu such a great fright the first night of their stay in Lansdale. Up one walk and down another they went—the boy whistling, laughing, capering about and the dog bounding after, catching up with his playfellow, and leaping upon him, now on this side and now on that, then, presently, finding himself shaken off and distanced in the race—but only for a moment. The next moment he was at the boy's side again or close at his heels.

"Max! Max!" called an eager child's voice, and Lulu came running down the path leading directly from the house.

"Well, what is it, Lu?" asked the lad, standing still to look and listen. "Down, Nero, down! Do be quiet, sir!"

"Oh, I have something to tell you," replied Lulu, breathlessly, as she hurried toward him. "That letter you brought Grandma Elsie from the post office this morning was from Aunt Elsie. They are at home by this time—she wrote just as they were ready to start—and Evelyn Leland is with them. She's to make her home at Fairview."

"Well, and what of it? What do I care about it? Or you, either?"

"Dear me, Max, you might care! I hope she may prove a nice friend for me—not a bit like Rosie who has always despised and disliked me."

"I don't think Rosie does anything of the kind, Lulu," said Max, patting Nero's head. "She may not be fond of you, and she certainly does not admire your behavior at times, but I don't believe it amounts to dislike."

"I do, then," returned Lulu—a touch of anger in her tones. "Anyhow, I'd dearly love to have a real friend near my own age, and Aunt Elsie says Evelyn is only a little older than I am."

"Well, I hope you won't be disappointed. If she was a boy I'd be as glad of her coming, or his coming, as you are."

"Oh, Maxie. I wish, for your sake, she was a boy!" cried Lulu in her impulsive way, stepping closer and putting her arm about his neck. "How selfish of me to forget that you have no companion at all at Ion!"

"I have," returned Max. "I have you, you know, and you're right good company when you are in a good humor."

"And I'm not often in any other with you, Maxie, now am I?" she said coaxingly.

"No, sis, that's true enough. And I do believe I couldn't get along half so well without you. I'm glad for your sake that this—what's her name?—is coming to live at Fairview."

"Her name is Evelyn. Oh, Max, I feel so very sorry for her!"

"Why?"

"Because her father's dead, and they were so very, very fond of each other—so Aunt Elsie wrote to Grandma Elsie."

"Rosie's father's dead, too, and she and all of them were very fond of him."

"Yes, but it's a good while now since he died, and she's had time to get over it so far that she seems hardly ever to think of him, while it is only a few weeks since Evelyn lost hers. And Rosie has her nice, kind mother with her, while Evelyn's is away in Europe and like enough isn't half so nice as Grandma Elsie anyhow. Oh, Max, I feel most heartbroken every time papa goes away, even though I expect to see him back again some day. Think how dreadful to have your father gone never to come back!"

"Yes, that would be awful!" said Max. "I'd rather lose ten years off my own life. But, Lu, if you really love papa so dearly, how can you behave toward him as you do sometimes—causing him so much distress of mind? I've seen such a grieved, troubled look on his face when he thought nobody was watching him, and you were in one of your naughty moods."

"Oh, Max, don't!" Lulu said in a choking voice as she turned and walked away—hot tears in her eyes.

Max ran after her. "Come, Lu, don't take it so hard. I didn't mean to be cruel."

"But you were! Go away! You've got me into one of my moods, as you call it, and I'd better be let alone," she returned almost fiercely. She jerked herself loose—for he had caught a fold of her dress in his hand—and rushing away to the farther end of the grounds, she threw herself on a rustic seat panting with excitement and the rapidity of her flight.

But the gust of passion died down almost as speedily as it had arisen. She could never be angry very long with Max, her dear, only brother. And now her thoughts turned remorsefully upon the conduct he had condemned. It was no news to her that she had more than once caused her father more anxiety and grief of heart, nor was it a new thing for her to be repentant and remorseful on account of her unfilial behavior.

"Oh, why can't I be as good as Max and Gracie?" she said to herself, covering her face with her hands and sighing heavily. "I wish papa was here so I could tell him again how sorry I am and how dearly I do love him, though I am so often naughty. I am glad I did tell him, and that he forgave me and told me he loved me just as well as any other of his children. How good of him to say that! I wonder if Evelyn Leland ever behaved badly to her father. If she ever was naughty to him, how sorry she must feel about it now!"

During the remainder of the short visit at Lansdale and all through the homeward journey, Lulu's thoughts often turned upon Evelyn. She had scarcely alighted from the carriage on their arrival at Ion before she sent a sweeping glance around the welcoming group on the veranda in eager search of the young stranger.

Yes, there she was, a little, slender girl in deep mourning dress, standing slightly apart from the embracing, rejoicing relatives. She was not decidedly pretty but graceful and refined in appearance. She had an earnest, intelligent countenance and very fine eyes. She seemed quite entirely free from self-consciousness and wholly taken up with the interest of the scenes being enacted before her.

"How many of them there are! And how they love one another! How nice it is!" she was thinking within herself when the two Elsies, releasing each other from a long, tender embrace, turned toward her, the older one saying, inquiringly, "And this must be Evelyn?"

"Yes, mamma. Eva, this is my dear mother," said Mrs. Leland.

Mrs. Travilla took the little girl in her arms, kissed her affectionately, and bade her welcome to Ion, adding, "If you like, you may call me Grandma Elsie as the others do."

Thank you, ma'am," Evelyn answered, coloring with pleasure. "But it seems hardly appropriate, for you look not very much older than Aunt Elsie, and she is very young to be my aunt."

"That's right, Eva," Mrs. Leland said with a pleased laugh. "I for one have never approved of mamma being called so by anyone older than my baby boy."

Mrs. Travilla's attention was claimed by someone else at that moment, and Lester, taking Evelyn by the hand, led her up to Mr. and Mrs. Dinsmore. She was introduced to the others in turn, everyone greeting her with the utmost kindness. Rosie gave her a hasty kiss, but Lulu embraced her with warmth, saying, "I am sure I shall love you, and I hope you will love me a little in return."

"I'll try. It wouldn't be fair to let it be all on one side," Evelyn answered with a shy, sweet smile, as she returned the hug and kiss as heartily as they were given.

Lulu was delighted.

After supper, while all of the older people were chatting busily among themselves, she drew Evelyn into a distant corner and told her how glad she was of her coming, because she wanted a girl friend near her own age and found Rosie uncongenial and indifferent toward her.

"She will probably be the same to me," said Evelyn. "She has so many of her own dear ones about her, you know, that it cannot be expected that she will feel much interest in strangers like you and me. But, frankly, I think I should love you best anyhow."

"How nice of you!" said Lulu, her eyes sparkling. "But I'm afraid you won't when you know me better, for I'm not a bit good. I get into terrible passions when anybody imposes on me or my brother or sister. And I sometimes disobey and break rules."

"You are very honest, at all events," remarked Evelyn pleasantly. "And perhaps I shall not like you any less for having some faults. You see, if you were perfect, the contrast between you and myself would be most unpleasant to me."

"How correctly and like a grownup person you speak!" said Lulu, regarding her new friend with affectionate admiration.

Evelyn's eyes filled. "It is because papa made me his constant companion and took the greatest pains with me," she said in tones tremulous with emotion. "We were almost always alone together—for I never had a brother or sister to share the love he lavished upon me."

"I'm so, so sorry for you!" said Lulu, slipping an arm round Evelyn's waist. "I think I know a little of how you feel. My papa is with us only once in a while for a few days or weeks, and when he goes away again it nearly breaks my heart."

"But you can hope he may come back again."

"Yes, and I have Max and Gracie, and that makes it so much easier to bear."

"And such a sweet, pretty mamma," supplemented Evelyn, sending an admiring glance across the room to where Violet sat chatting with her sister Elsie.

"But you have your own mother, and that's a great deal better," returned Lulu. "Mamma Vi is very beautiful, sweet, and very kind to Max, Gracie, and me, but a stepmother can't be like your own."

"I suppose not quite," Evelyn said with a sigh. "But I have no idea when I shall see mine again."

"We are situated a good deal alike," remarked Lulu, reflectively. "My father and your mother are far away in this world, and your father and my mother are gone to heaven."

"Yes. Oh, don't you sometimes want to go to them there?"

"I'm not good enough—not fit in any way. And I believe I'd rather stay here—at least while papa does," Lulu said with some hesitation.

"I hope he may be spared to you for many, many years," said Evelyn gently. "I pray at least till you are quite grown up and perhaps have a family and children of your own."

"Were you ever so naughty that your father told you that you gave him a great deal of trouble and heartache?" asked Lulu in a tremulous voice and with starting tears.

"No, indeed!" exclaimed Eva in surprise. "How could I, or anyone, with such a father as mine?"

"No father could be better or kinder than mine," said Lulu, twinkling away a tear. "And yet I have been so passionate and disobedient that he has told me that several times."

"Oh, don't ever be so again. If you do your poor heart will ache so terribly over it when he is taken away from you," Evelyn said with emotion, pressing Lulu's hand affectionately in hers. "Oh, I can never be thankful enough," she went on, "that the day my dear father was called home he said to me, 'My darling, you have been nothing but a blessing and comfort to me since the day you were born.'"

"My father can never say that to me. I have already put it out of his power," thought Lulu to herself with a great pain in her heart. As soon as she found herself quite alone in her own room that night, she wrote a little penitent note to him all blistered with tears.

Shortly after breakfast the next morning Lulu went to Grandma Elsie with a request for her permission to walk over to Fairview and spend an hour with Evelyn.

"You may, my dear, if you can get Max or some older person to walk with you," was Elsie's kind reply. "Otherwise, I will send you in the carriage, because it is not safe for you to walk that distance alone. I think you and Evelyn are going to be friends, and I am very glad of it," she added with a pleasant smile. "If she will come, you may bring her back with you to spend the day at Ion."

"Oh, thank you, Grandma Elsie. That will be so nice!" cried Lulu, joyously. Then she bounded away in search of her brother.

Max, having nothing else to do just then, readily consented to be Lulu's escort, and the two set out for Fairview at once.

"A brother is of some use sometimes, isn't he?" queried Max complacently as they walked briskly down the avenue together.

"Yes, and isn't a sister, too?" asked Lulu.

"Yes, indeed," he said. "You are almost always ready to do me a good turn, Lu. But, in fact, I'm taking this walk quite as much to please myself as you. It's a very pleasant one on a morning like this, and Uncle Lester and Aunt Elsie are very pleasant folks to visit."

"I think they are," returned Lulu. "But I am going more to see Evelyn than anybody else. Oh, Max, I do hope, I do believe, it's going to be as I told you I wished it would be."

"What?"

"That we'll be intimate friends and very fond of each other. Weren't you very pleased with her, Max? I was."

"She's nice looking," he replied. "But that's all I can say till we've had time to get acquainted."

"I feel quite well acquainted with her now. We had such a nice, long talk together last night," said Lulu.

Evelyn was strolling about the grounds at Fairview and came to the gate to meet them. She shook hands with Max, kissed Lulu affectionately, and invited them into the house.

They settled themselves on the veranda, where Mrs. Leland presently joined the little trio. Then Lulu gave Grandma Elsie's invitation for Evelyn to spend the day at Ion.

"May I go, Aunt Elsie?" asked Evelyn.

"Certainly, dear, if you wish to," Mrs. Leland answered kindly. Your uncle and I will drive over early in the evening and bring you home."

"By moonlight!" Evelyn cried. "That will be very nice. Auntie, you and uncle are very good to me."

"Indeed, child," returned Elsie, smiling, "you may well believe it is no hardship for us to go to Ion on any errand — or with none save the desire to see mamma and the rest."

Evelyn and Lulu passed the greater part of the day alone together — everyone else seemingly lacking either the leisure or inclination to join them. The friendship grew rapidly, as is usually the case when two little girls are thus thrown together.

Each gave a detailed history of her past life and found the other deeply interested in it. Then they talked of the present and the near future.

"Are you to go to school?" asked Lulu.

"No," Evelyn said with a contented smile. "I am to study at home and come here to recite with you."

"Oh, how nice!" cried Lulu, her eyes sparkling with pleasure.

"Yes, I think it very kind of Aunt Elsie's mother and grandfather to offer to let me do so," said Evelyn. "I shall try very hard to be studious and well-behaved and give them no trouble."

Lulu's cheeks flushed at that remark, and for a moment she sat silent and with downcast eyes. Then she burst out in her impetuous way, "I wish I were like you, Eva — so good and grateful. I'm afraid you wouldn't care for me at all if you knew what a bad, ungrateful thing I am. I've given ever so much trouble to Grandpa Dinsmore and Grandma Elsie, though they have done more for me — for Max and Gracie, too — than they are going to do for you."

"I don't believe you're half so bad as you make yourself out to be," returned Eva in a surprised tone. "And I'm sure you are sorry and will be ever so good and grateful in the future."

"I want to, but—there does seem to be no use in my trying to be sweet-tempered and all that," said Lulu dejectedly. "I've got such a dreadful temper."

"Papa used to tell me that God, our heavenly Father, would help me to conquer my faults if I asked Him with all my heart," said Evelyn softly. "Papa said that in His great love and condescension, He noticed even a little child and his efforts to please Him and do His will."

"Yes, I know. My papa has told me the same thing ever so often, but 'most always the temptation comes so suddenly, I don't seem to have time to ask for help, and—oh, I'm ashamed to admit it—sometimes I don't want it, Eva."

CHAPTER ELEVENTH

*O blessed, happy child, to find
The God of heaven so near and kind!*

KIT WAS SUNDAY afternoon, and in the large dining room at Ion, a Bible reading was being held. Mr. Dinsmore was leading, and every member of the household, down to the servants who occupied the lower end of the apartment, were bearing a share in the exercises. Lester, Elsie, and Evelyn from Fairview, representatives from the other three families belonging to the larger family connection, and the Keith cousins who had arrived at Ion a few days before—all were present.

The portion of Scripture under consideration was the interview of Nicodemus with the Master when he came to Him by night which is found in John, chapter three. The subject, of course, was the necessity of the new birth, God's appointed way of salvation, and the exceeding greatness of His love in giving His only begotten Son to die "that whosoever believeth in Him should not perish, but have everlasting life."

Each one able to read had an open Bible in their laps, and even Gracie and little Walter listened with both understanding and interest.

She whom the one called mamma, the other Grandma Elsie, had talked with them that morning on the same subject and tenderly urged upon them—as often before—the duty of coming to Christ. She told them of His love to little children, and that they were not too young to give themselves to Him. Mr. Dinsmore addressed a few closing words to them in the same strain.

They fell into Gracie's heart as seed sown in good soil. When the reading had come to an end and she felt herself unobserved, she slipped quietly away to her mamma's dressing room, where she was not likely to be disturbed, and sat down to think more profoundly and seriously than ever before in her short life.

She went over "the old, old story," and tears stole down her cheeks as she whispered to herself. "And it was for me He died that dreadful death, for me just as truly as if it hadn't been for anybody else. Yet I've lived all this long while without loving Him or trying to do right for the sake of pleasing Him.

"And how often I've been invited to come! Papa has told me about it over and over again, mamma, too, and Grandma Elsie. And I haven't minded what they said at all. Oh, how patient and kind Jesus has been to wait so long for me to come! And He is still waiting and inviting me to come—just as kindly and lovingly as if it was the very first time, and I hadn't been turning away from Him.

"He is right here, looking at me and listening for what I will say in answer to His call. Oh, I won't keep Him waiting any longer, lest He should go away and never invite me again. I do so love Him for dying for me and for being so good and kind to me all my life—giving me every blessing I have. He has kept on inviting me, over and over, when I wouldn't even listen to His voice.

"I'll go to Him now. Grandma Elsie said just to kneel down and feel that I am kneeling at His feet. She said I should tell Him all about my sins, and how sorry I am—exactly as if I could see Him, and ask Him to forgive my sins and wash them all away in His precious blood. She also said I should ask him to take me for His very own child to be His forever and to serve Him always in this world and in heaven when He takes me there. Yes, I will heed the call and do it now."

With that firm resolve she rose from the chair where she had been sitting. She knelt before it with clasped hands and closed eyes, from which penitent tears stole down her cheeks, and said in low, reverent tones, "Dear Lord Jesus, I'm only a little girl and very full of sin. I've done a great many bad things in my life and haven't done the good things I knew I ought to do. I have a very bad heart that doesn't want to do right. Oh, please make it good. Oh, please take away all the wickedness that is in me and wash me in Thy precious blood so that I shall be clean and pure in Thy sight. Forgive me for living so long without loving Thee, when I've known all the time about Thy great love to me. Help me to love Thee now and forever more. I give myself to Thee to be all Thine forever and forever. Amen."

Her prayer was ended, yet she did not at once rise from her kneeling posture. It was so sweet a place to linger there at the Master's feet. She remembered and trusted His promise, "Him that cometh to Me I will in no wise cast out," and she could almost hear in her ears His dear voice saying in tenderest tones, "Daughter, thy sins, which are many, are forgiven thee."

"I love them that love Me, and those that seek Me early shall find Me."

She seemed to feel the touch of His hand laid in blessing on her head, and her heart sang for joy.

Meanwhile, the older children had gathered about Aunt Chloe, who was now seated on a back veranda. The weather was still warm enough for the outer air to be very pleasant at that time of day, and Rosie, as spokesman of the party, begged her coaxingly for stories of mamma when she was a little girl.

"It's de Lawd's day, chillens," answered the old woman in a doubtful tone.

"Yes, mammy," acknowledged Rosie. "But you can easily make your story fit for Sunday. Mamma was so good—a real Christian child, as you have often told me."

"So she was, chile. So she was. I's sho' she lub de Lawd from de bery day her ole mammy fus' tole her how He lub her. Yes, you right, Miss Rosie, I kin tole you 'bout her, and 'twon't break de Sabbath day. Is yo' all hyar now?" she asked, glancing inquiringly about.

"All but Gracie," said Rosie, glancing round the little circle in her turn. "I wonder where she is. Betty, please go and find Miss Gracie and ask if she doesn't want to hear the stories mammy is going to tell us."

"Yes, Miss Rosie. Whar you s'pose Miss Gracie done gone?" drawled the little maid, standing quite still and pulling at one of the short braids scattered here and there over her head.

"I don't know. Go and look for her," returned Rosie, somewhat imperiously. "Now hurry," she added. "Or there won't be time for all mammy has to tell."

"Wisht I know whar Miss Gracie done gone," sighed Betty, reluctantly obeying.

"I saw her going upstairs," said Lulu. "So it's likely you'll find her in Mamma Vi's rooms."

At that, Betty quickened her pace, and the next moment was at Violet's dressing room door, peeping in and asking, "You dar, Miss Gracie?"

"Yes," Gracie answered, turning toward her a face so full of gladness that Betty's eyes opened wide in astonishment. Stepping in, she asked in wonder, "What—what de mattah, Miss Gracie? Yo' look like yo' done gone foun' a gol' mine, or jes' sumfin' mos' like dat."

"Better still, Betty. I've found the Lord Jesus. I love Him, and He loves me," Gracie said, her eyes shining brightly. "And oh, I am so glad, so happy!"

"Whar yo' fin' Him, Miss Gracie?" queried Betty in increasing wonder and astonishment, glancing searchingly round the room. "Is He hyar?"

"Yes, for He is God and is everywhere."

"Oh, dat de way He hyar? Yes, I knows 'bout dat. Miss Elsie tole me lots ob times. How yo' know He lub yo', Miss Gracie?"

"Because He says so, Betty. 'Jesus loves me, this I know, for the Bible tells me so.'"

"Yo's wanted downstairs on de back veranda, Miss Gracie," said Betty, reminding herself of her errand. "Ole Aunt Chloe gwine tell 'bout de old times when missus bery little and lib way off down Souf. Bettah come right 'long, kase Miss Rosie she in pow'ful big hurry fo' Aunt Chloe begin dat story."

"Oh, yes. I never get tired of hearing mammy tell that. Grandma Elsie was such a dear little girl," Gracie said, making haste to obey the summons.

The others had already gathered closely about Aunt Chloe, but the circle promptly widened to receive Gracie. The moment she had taken her seat the story began, opening with the birth of its subject.

There were many little reminiscences of her infancy and early childhood that were very interesting to all the listeners. The narrator dwelt at length upon the evidences of early piety shown in the child's life, and Aunt Chloe remarked, "Yo' needn't be 'fraid, chillens, ob bein' too good to lib. My darlin' was de bes' chile eber I see, and yo' know she has lib to see her chillen and her gran'chillens."

"I'm not at all afraid of it," remarked Rosie. "People who are certainly don't know or don't believe what the Bible teaches on that point, for it says, 'My son, forget not My law; but let thine heart keep My commandments; for length of days and long life, and peace shall they add to thee.'"

"And there's a promise of both long life and prosperity to all who keep the fifth commandment," said Max.

"'So far as it shall serve for God's glory and their own good,'" added Evelyn softly.

"Dat's so, chillens," said Aunt Chloe. "An' yo' ole mammy hopes ebery one ob yo's gwine try it all de days ob yo' life."

"Yes, we're goin' to, mammy. So now tell us some more," begged Walter coaxingly. "Tell about the time when the poor little girl that's my mamma now had to go away and leave her pretty home."

"Yaas, chile, dat wur a sad time," said the old woman reflectively. "It mos' broke de little chile's heart to hab to leab dat home whar she been borned, an' all de dear ones dat lub her like dar life."

She went on to describe the parting, then to tell of the journey, and was just beginning with the life at Roselands when the summons came to the tea table.

"We'll come back to hear the rest after tea, mammy, if you're not too tired," Rosie said as she turned to go.

But on coming back they found no one on the veranda but Betty, who, in answer to their inquiries, said, "Aunt Chloe hab entired fo' de night. She hab de misery in de back and in de head, and she cayn't tell no mo' stories fo' mawning."

"Poor old soul!" said Evelyn, compassionately. "I'm afraid we've tired her out."

"Oh no, not at all," answered Rosie. "She likes nothing better than talking about mamma. You never saw anything like her devotion. I verily believe she'd die for mamma without even a moment's hesitation."

Most of the house servants at Ion occupied cabins of their own at no great distance from the mansion, but Aunt Chloe, the faithful nurse of three generations, was domiciled in a most comfortable apartment not far from those of the mistress to whom she was so dear. And Elsie never laid her own head upon its pillow till she had paid a visit to mammy's room to see that she wanted for nothing that could contribute to ease of body or mind.

This night, stealing softly in, she found her lying with closed eyes and hands meekly folded across her breast, and, thinking she slept, would have gone away again as quietly as she came, but the loved voice recalled her.

"Dat yo', honey? Don' go. Yo' ole mammy's got somefin to say, and de time is short 'kase the chariot wheels dey's rollin' fas'—fas' dis way to carry yo' ole mammy home to glory."

"Dear mammy," Elsie said with emotion, laying her hand tenderly on the sable brow. "Are you feeling weaker or in any way worse than usual?"

"Dunno, honey, but I hear de Master callin' an' I's ready to follow whereber He leads—eben down into de valley ob de shadow ob death. I's close to de riber. I's hear de soun' ob de wattahs ripplin' pas', but de eberlastin' arms is underneath, an' I sho' to git safe ober to de oder side."

"Yes, dear mammy, I know you will," Elsie answered in moved tones. "I know you will come off more than conqueror through Him who loved you with an everlasting love."

"'Peat dat verse to yo' ole mammy, honey," entreated the trembling, feeble voice.

"What verse, my mammy dear? The 'Who shall separate us'?"

"Yes, darlin', dat's it! An' de res' dat comes after, whar de 'postle say he 'suaded dat deff nor nuffin else cayn't separate God's chillen from de love ob Christ."

Elsie complied, adding at the close of the lengthy quotation, "Such precious words! How often you and I have rejoiced over them together, mammy!"

"'Deed we hab, honey. An' we's gwine rejoice in dem togeder beside de great white throne. Now yo' go an' take yo' res', darlin', an' de Lawd gib yo' sweet sleep."

"I can't leave you, mammy, if you are suffering. You must let me sit beside you and do what is in my power to relieve your pain or help you to forget it."

"No, chile, no. De miseries am all gone an' Ise mighty comfor'able. Ise bery happy, too, hearin' de soun' ob de chariot wheels and tinking I's soon be in de bressed lan' whar de miseries an' de sins am all done gone foreber an' whar ole Uncle Joe an' de bressed Master is waitin' to 'ceive me wid songs of joy and gladness."

Thus reassured and perceiving no symptom of approaching dissolution, Elsie returned to her own apartments and was soon in bed and asleep.

In accordance with an old Ion rule which Lulu particularly disliked, the children had gone to their rooms an hour or more in advance of the older people.

Gracie still slept with her mamma in her father's absence but often made her preparations for bed in her sister's room, that they might chat freely together of whatever was uppermost in their minds.

Tonight they were no sooner shut in there, away from other eyes, than Gracie put her arms round Lulu's neck, saying, as her face shone with gladness, "Oh, Lu, I have something to tell you!"

"Have you?" Lulu answered. "Then it must be something good—for in all your life I never saw you look so very, very happy. Oh, is it news from papa? Is he coming home on another visit?" she cried with a sudden, eager lighting up of her face.

The brightness of Gracie's dimmed a trifle as she replied, "No, not that. They would never let him come again so soon. I wish he was here. He would be so glad of it, too! Almost as glad as I am, I think."

"Glad of what?" asked Lulu.

"That I've given my heart to Jesus. Oh, Lulu, won't you do it, too? It is so very, very easy if you only just try."

"Tell me about it. How did you do it?" Lulu asked gravely. Her eyes were cast down, a slight frown was upon her brow.

"I did just as Grandma Elsie told us this morning. You know, Lu?"

"Yes, I remember. But how do you know that you were heard and accepted?"

"Why, Lulu!" was the surprised reply. "The Bible tells us God is the hearer and answerer of prayer — it's in one of the verses I've learned to say to Grandma Elsie since I came here. And Jesus says: 'Him that cometh unto Me I will in no wise cast out,' so of course He received me. How could I help knowing it?"

"You've gotten far ahead of me," Lulu said with petulance born of an uneasy conscience. She released herself from Gracie's arms and began undressing with great energy and dispatch.

"You needn't feel that way, Lu," Gracie said pleadingly. "Jesus is just as willing to take you for His child as me."

"I don't believe it!" cried Lulu with almost fierce impatience. "You've always been good, and I've always been bad. I don't see why I wasn't made patient and sweet-tempered, too. It's no trouble to you to behave and keep rules and all that, but I can't. Try as hard as I will, I can't!"

"Oh, Lulu, Jesus will help you to be good if you ask Him and try as hard as you can, too," Gracie said in tender, pleading tones.

"But suppose I don't want to be good?"

Gracie's eyes opened wide in grieved surprise, then filled with tears. "Oh, Lulu!" she cried. "But I'm sure you do want to be good sometimes. And can't Jesus help you to want to always? Won't He if you ask Him?"

"I'm tired of the subject, and it's time for you to go to bed," came the ungracious rejoinder.

Usually so unkind a rebuff from her sister would have caused Gracie a fit of crying, but she was too happy for that tonight. She slipped quietly into her mamma's rooms, and when ready for bed she came to the door again with a pleasant "Good night, Lulu, and happy dreams!"

Lulu, already repentant, sprang to meet her with usual outstretched arms. "Good night, you dear little thing!" she exclaimed with a hug and a kiss. "I wish you had a better sort of a sister. Perhaps you will some day—in little Elsie."

"I love you dearly, Lu!" came the affectionate rejoinder, accompanied by a hearty return of the fond embrace.

"I wish mamma would come up. I want to tell her, 'cause I know it will make her glad, too," Gracie said to herself as she got into bed. "I mean to stay awake till she comes."

When Violet finally came into the room she stepped softly to the bedside and bent over the sleeping child, gazing with tender scrutiny into the fair, young face.

"The darling!" she murmured. "What a sweet and peaceful expression she wears! I noticed it several times during the evening—a look as if some great good had come to her."

A very gentle kiss was laid upon the child's forehead, and Violet passed on into Lulu's room, moved by a motherly solicitude to see that all was well with this one of her husband's children also.

The face that rested on the pillow was round and rosy with youth and health. The brow was unruffled, yet the countenance lacked the exceeding sweet expression of her sister's.

Violet kissed her also, and Lulu, half opening her sleepy eyes, murmured, "Mamma Vi, you're very good and kind." And with the last word she was fast asleep again.

⚶ ⚶ ⚶ ⚶ ⚶

Mrs. Elsie Travilla rose earlier the next morning than her wont—a vague uneasiness oppressing her in regard to her aged nurse. Waiting only to don dressing gown and slippers, she went softly to Aunt Chloe's bedside. Finding her sleeping quite peacefully, she returned as quietly as she had come, thinking to pay another visit before descending to the breakfast room.

Only a few minutes had passed, however, when the little maid Betty came rushing in unceremoniously, her eyes wild with fright. "Missus, missus," she cried, "suffin de mattah wid ole Aunt Chloe. She—she—"

Elsie waited to hear no more, but pushing past the child, flew to the rescue.

One glance at the aged face told her that no human help could avail. The seal of death was on it.

A great wave of sorrow swept over her at the sight, but she was outwardly calm and composed as, taking the cold hand in hers, she asked, "Dear mammy, is it peace?"

"Yes, chile, yes," came in feeble yet assured accents from the dying lips. "An' I's almos' dar—a po' ole sinnah saved by grace. Good-bye, honey, we's meet again at de Master's feet, neber to part no mo'!"

One or two long-drawn gasping breaths followed, and the aged pilgrim had entered into rest.

At the same instant a strong arm was passed round Elsie's waist, while a manly voice said tenderly, "We will not grieve for her, dear daughter—for all her pains, all her troubles are over, and she has been gathered home like a shock of corn fully ripe."

"Yes, dear father, but let me weep a little—not for her, but for myself," Elsie said, allowing him to draw her head to a resting place upon his shoulder.

In the meanwhile, both Violet and Gracie had awakened from sleep, and the little girl had told of her newfound happiness, meeting with the joyful sympathy she had expected.

"Dear Gracie," Violet said, taking the little girl in her arms and kissing her tenderly, "you are a blessed, happy child in having so early chosen the better part which shall never be taken away from you. Jesus will be your friend all your life, be it long or short. He will be a friend that sticketh closer than a brother, who will never leave nor forsake you, but will love you with an everlasting love more tender than a mother's and be always near and mighty to help and save in every time of trouble and distress."

"Oh, mamma," said Gracie, "how good and kind He is to let me love Him! I wish I could do something to please Him. What could I do, mamma?"

"He said to His disciples, 'If ye love Me, keep My commandments,' and He says the same to you and me, Gracie, dear," Violet answered.

"I will try, mamma, and won't you help me?"

"All I can, dear. Now it is time for us to rise."

They had nearly completed getting dressed when a tap at the door was followed by the entrance of Violet's mother, looking grave and sad and with traces of tears about her eyes.

"Mamma, what is it?" Violet asked anxiously.

"Our dear old mammy is gone, daughter," Elsie answered, the tears beginning to fall again. "She is gone home to glory. I do not weep for her, but for myself. You know what she was to me."

"Yes, mamma, dearest. I am very sorry for you, but for her it should be all joy, should it not? Life can have been little but a burden to her for some years past, and now she is at God's right hand where there are pleasures forevermore."

Elsie assented and sat down, giving a full account of what had passed between Aunt Chloe and herself the previous night and of the death scene this morning.

"What a long, long journey hers has been!" remarked Violet. "But she has reached home at last. And here, mamma," drawing Gracie forward, "is a new little pilgrim who has but just passed through the wicket-gate and begun to travel the straight and narrow way."

"Is it so, Gracie? It makes my heart glad to hear it," Elsie said, taking the child in her arms in a tender, motherly fashion. "You are none too young to begin to love and serve the Lord Jesus, and it's a blessed service. I found it such when I was a child like you, and such I have found it all the way that I have travailed since."

❧❧❧❧❧❧

CHAPTER TWELFTH

Lulu Rebels

SEVERAL WEEKS HAD passed since the events of Aunt Chloe's passing, during which life had moved on its accustomed way at Fairview and Ion.

Evelyn was as happy in her new home as she could have been anywhere without her father and mother—perhaps happier than she would have been anywhere with the latter—and enjoyed her studies under Mr. Dinsmore's tutelage. Being very steady, respectful, studious, and in every way a well-behaved child, and also an interested pupil, she found favor with him. She was never subjected to reproof or punishment, but she was smiled upon and constantly commended. In consequence her opinion of him differed widely from that of Lulu, whose quick, willful temper was continually getting her into trouble with him.

She was the only one of his scholars who caused him any serious annoyance. He had grown weary of contending with her, and one day when she had failed in her recitation and answered impertinently his well-merited reproof, he said to her, "Lucilla, you may leave the room and consider yourself banished from it for a week. At the end of that time, I shall probably be able to decide whether I will ever again listen to a recitation from you."

Lulu, with cheeks aflame and eyes flashing, hardly waited for the conclusion of the sentence ere she rose and rushed from the room, shutting the door behind her with a loud slam.

Mr. Dinsmore stepped to it and called her back.

"I desire you to come in here again and then leave us in a proper and ladylike manner, closing the door quietly," he said.

For a single instant Lulu hesitated, strongly tempted to refuse obedience, but even she stood in some awe of Mr. Dinsmore, and seeing his stern, determined look, she retraced her steps. With head erect and eyes that carefully avoided the faces of all present, she went quietly out again, closed the door gently, then hurried through the hall, down the stairs, and into her own room. There she hastily donned hat and coat and rapidly descended to the ground floor. The next instant she might have been seen fairly flying down the avenue.

Her passion had slightly cooled by the time she reached the gate, and giving up her first intention of passing through into the road beyond, she turned into an alley bordered by evergreens which would screen her from view from the house. There she paced back and forth, muttering angrily to herself between her shut teeth.

"I hate him, so I do! The old tyrant! He's no business to give me such long, hard lessons and scold because I couldn't recite perfectly."

Her conscience gently reminded her that she could easily have mastered her task if her time had not been wasted over a storybook.

"It's a pity if I can't have the pleasure of reading a story once in a while," she said in reply to the stick. "And I'm not going to give up doing it either for him or anybody else. He reads stories himself, and if it's bad, it's worse for grown folks than for children. Oh, how I do wish I was grown up and could do just as I please!"

Then came to mind her father's assurance that even grown people could not always follow their own inclinations. She was also reminded of his expressions of deep gratitude to Mr. Dinsmore and Grandma Elsie for giving his children a home with them and taking the trouble to teach and train them up for useful and happy lives. Lulu well knew that Mr. Dinsmore received no compensation for his labors in behalf of her brother and sister and herself, and that few people would be at such pains for no other reward than consciousness of doing good. Reflecting upon all this, she at length began to feel really ashamed of her bad behavior.

Yet pride prevented her from fully acknowledging it even in her own heart. But recalling the doubt he had expressed as to whether he would ever again hear a recitation from her, she began to feel very uneasy as to what might be the consequences to her of such a refusal on his part.

Her education must go on—that she knew. But who would be her teacher if Mr. Dinsmore refused? In all probability she would be sent away to the much dreaded boarding school. Indeed she felt quite certain of it in case the question should be referred to her father. Had he not warned her that if she were troublesome or disobedient to Mr. Dinsmore, such would be her fate?

A fervent wish arose that he might not be appealed to—might forever be left in ignorance of this her latest act of insubordination. She would, it was true, have to make a report to him of the day's conduct, but she could refrain from telling the whole story — could smooth the matter over so that he would not understand how extremely impertinent and passionate she had been.

Everything that had passed between Mr. Dinsmore and herself had been seen and heard by all her fellow pupils, and the thought of that did not tend to lessen Lulu's mortification and dread of the consequences.

"Rosie will treat me more than ever like the Pharisee did the publican," she said bitterly to herself. "Max and Gracie will be ashamed of their sister; Walter will look at me as if he thought me the worst girl alive; and perhaps Evelyn won't be my friend any more. Mr. Dinsmore will act as if he didn't see me at all, I suppose, and Grandma Elsie and Aunt Elsie and Mamma Vi will be grave and sad. Oh dear, I 'most think I'm willing to go to boarding school to get away from it all!"

Evelyn had been greatly shocked and surprised at Lulu's outburst of temper — for she had become strongly attached to her and had not known her to be capable of such an exhibition of passion.

During the scene in the schoolroom, Rosie sent angry glances at Lulu, but Evelyn sat silent with eyes cast down, unwilling to witness her friend's disgrace. Max hid his face with his book, Gracie wept, and little Walter looked on in silent astonishment.

"She is the most ill-tempered piece I ever saw!" remarked Rosie, aloud, as the door closed upon Lulu for the second time.

"Rosie," said her grandfather sternly, "let me hear no more such observations from your lips. They are entirely uncalled for and extremely uncharitable, young lady."

Rosie reddened and did not venture to speak again, or even to so much as raise her eyes from her book for some time.

The outdoor air was quite keen and cold, and Lulu was beginning to feel chilled. She was debating in her own mind whether to return at once to the house in spite of the danger of meeting someone who knew of her disgrace and was therefore likely to look at her askance, when a light, quick step approached her from behind and two arms suddenly were thrown around her neck.

"Oh, Lu. Dear Lu," said Evelyn's soft voice. "I am so, so sorry!"

"Eva! I did not think you would come to find me. Do you really care for me still?" asked Lulu in quiet, subdued tones as she averted her face.

"Of course I do. Did you suppose I was not a true friend that would stand by you in both trouble and disgrace as well as when all goes prosperously with you?"

"But it was my own fault for not learning my lesson better in the first place and then answering Grandpa Dinsmore as I did when he reproved me," said Lulu, hanging her head. "I know papa would say so if he were here and punish me severely, too."

"Still I'm sorry for you," Eva repeated. "I'm not, by any means, always good myself. I might have neglected my lessons under the same temptation, and if my temper were naturally as hot as yours I don't know that I should have been any more meek and respectful than you were under so sharp a rebuke, Lulu."

"It's very good of you to say it. You're not a bit of a Pharisee, but I think Rosie is very much like the one the Bible tells about—the one who thought himself so much better than the poor publican."

"Isn't it just possible you may be a little hard on Rosie?" suggested Eva with some hesitation, fearing to rouse the ungovernable temper again.

But Lulu did not show any anger. "I don't think I am," she replied quite calmly. "What did she say after I left the room?"

Eva was very averse to tale bearing, so merely answered the query with another. "Why do you suppose she said anything?"

"Because I know her of old. She dislikes and despises me, and she seems ready to express her sentiments whenever the slightest occasion offers."

"That reminds me," said Evelyn. "Just before he dismissed us, Grandpa Dinsmore requested us to refrain from mentioning what had passed, unless it should become quite necessary to do so."

"You may be sure Rosie will find it necessary," Lulu said. "She will tell her mamma all about it—Mamma Vi, too—and it will presently be known all over the house, even by the Keiths. I wish they weren't here."

"Don't you like them? I do."

"Yes, I think Aunt Marcia and Aunt Annis—as we children all call them—are kind and pleasant as can be. But I'd rather they wouldn't hear about this, though I gues I don't care so very much either," she added defiantly. "What difference does it make what people think of you, anyway?"

"Some difference, surely," said Evelyn gently. "The Bible says, 'A good name is rather to be chosen than riches, and loving favor rather than silver and gold.' Papa used to tell me that to deserve a good name and to have it, was one of the greatest blessings of life. I must go now," she added, pulling out a pretty little watch—one of the last gifts of that loved father. "Aunt Elsie will be expecting me."

"I wish I could go with you," said Lulu, sighing.

"Oh, that would be nice!" exclaimed Evelyn. "Can't you?"

Lulu shook her head. "Not without leave, and I don't want to ask it now. Oh, Eva, I do wish I didn't have to obey these people who are no relation to me!"

"But they are very kind, and Aunt Violet is your father's wife and loves you for his sake, I am sure."

"But she's too young to be a real mother to me, and the rest are no relation at all. I begged papa not to say I must, but he said it just the same."

"Then, loving him so dearly, as I am sure you do, I should think you would be quite willing to obey, because it is his will that you should."

"I don't see that that follows," grumbled Lulu. "And—now you will think me very bad, I know. I have sometimes even refused to obey papa himself."

"Oh, how sorry you will be for it if ever he is taken from you!" Eva said with emotion. "But did he let you have your own way?"

"No, indeed; he is as strict in exacting obedience from his children as Grandpa Dinsmore himself. I'm dreadfully afraid Grandpa Dinsmore or somebody will write to him about today. I do hope they won't, for he said if I should be disobedient and troublesome he would take me away from here and put me in a boarding school."

"And you wouldn't like that?"

"No, indeed! For how could I bear to be separated from Gracie and Max?"

"I hope you won't have to go. I should be sorry enough on my own account as a well as yours,"

Evelyn said with an affectionate kiss. "I must really go now, so good-bye, dear, till tomorrow."

Evelyn had hardly gone when Max joined his sister. "Lulu, why can't you behave?" he exclaimed in a tone of impatience and chagrin. "You make me and Gracie both ashamed of your ingratitude to Grandpa Dinsmore."

"I don't choose to be lectured by you, Max," returned Lulu with a toss of her head.

"No, but what do you suppose papa would say to this morning's behavior?"

"Suppose you write and tell him all about it, and see what he says," she returned scornfully.

"You know I must not do such a thing," said Max. "But I should think you would feel bound to do it."

"I intend to some day," she answered humbly. "But I don't think I need to just now. 'Tisn't likely he'd get the story anyhow for weeks or months."

"Well, you'll do your own way, but if it was my case, I'd rather confess and have it off my mind."

So saying, Max turned and walked toward the house, Lulu slowly following.

She quite dreaded meeting anyone belonging to the family, but she was already too thoroughly chilled to think of staying out another moment. She also knew that her misconduct could not be hidden from the family. They would notice that she did not go into the schoolroom, and they would see by Mr. Dinsmore's manner that she was in disgrace with him. So, to remain longer out in the cold was only delaying for a little while the ordeal which she must face sooner or later. Therefore, she rejoiced when she succeeded in gaining her own room without meeting anyone.

CHAPTER THIRTEENTH

What's done we partly may compute,
But know not what's resisted.

—BURNS

POOR, LITTLE GRACIE was sorely distressed over both her sister's misconduct and the consequent displeasure of Mr. Dinsmore.

On being dismissed from the schoolroom, she went directly to her mamma's apartments. She knew she would be alone there as Violet had gone driving, and shutting herself in, she indulged in a hearty cry.

She was aware of the danger that Lulu would be sent away, and she could not bear the thought of separation from her—the only sister she had except the baby.

Their mutual love was very strong. And Lulu was ever ready to act as Gracie's champion, did anyone show the slightest disposition to impose upon or ill-treat her. It was seldom indeed that she herself was anything but the kindest of the kind to her.

Finding her young stepmother ever ready with sympathy and help, too, where that was possible, Gracie had long since formed the habit of carrying to her all her little troubles and vexations and also all her joys.

She longed to open her heart now to "mamma," but Mr. Dinsmore's parting injunction as he dismissed his pupils for the day seemed to forbid it. Gracie felt that even that partial relief was now denied her.

But Violet came suddenly upon her and surprised her in the midst of her tears.

"Why darling, what is the matter?" she asked in a tone full of concern, taking the little girl in her arms.

"Oh, mamma, it's— But I mustn't tell you, 'cause Grandpa Dinsmore said we were not to mention it unless it was quite necessary."

"But surely you may tell your mamma anything that distresses you so! Is it that Grandpa Dinsmore is displeased?"

"Not with me, mamma."

"Then with Max or Lulu?"

"Mamma, I think I may tell you a little," Gracie replied, with some hesitation. "It's with Lulu, but I can't say what for. But, oh, mamma, if Grandpa Dinsmore won't teach Lu anymore, will she have to go away to a boarding school?"

"I hope not, dearie. I think not if she will be content to take me for her teacher," Violet said with a suppressed sigh—for she felt that she might be pledging herself to a most trying work. Lulu would dare much more in the way of disregarding her authority than that of her grandfather.

She was rewarded by Gracie's glad exclamation, "Oh, mamma, how good you are! I hope Lulu would never be naughty to you. How could she if you save her from being sent away?"

"I think Lulu wants to be good," Violet replied gently. "But she finds her naturally quick temper very hard to govern."

"But she always grows sorry very soon," Gracie remarked in a supplicating tone.

"Yes, dear, so she does. She is a dear child, and one cannot help loving her in spite of her faults."

"Thank you, mamma, for saying that!" Gracie exclaimed, throwing her arms round Violet's neck and kissing her cheek. "May I tell Lulu that you will teach her if Grandpa Dinsmore will not?"

"No, Gracie," Violet answered with grave look and tone. "It will do her good, I think, to fear for a while that she may lose the privileges she enjoys here by not valuing them enough to make good use of them or by indulging in improper behavior toward those whom her father has placed over her. Those who are in every way worthy of her respect and obedience."

"Yes, mamma," Gracie responded submissively.

"Where is Lulu?" Violet asked.

"I don't know. Oh yes, I see her coming up the avenue," she corrected herself as she glanced from a window. "She's been taking a walk, I s'pose."

Presently they heard Lulu enter her own room, shut the door, lock and bolt it, as if determined to secure herself from intrusion. But Gracie hastened to join her, passing through the door that opened from Violet's apartments.

Lulu, who was taking off her hat, turned sharply around with an angry frown on her brow. But it vanished at sight of the intruder.

"Oh, it's only you, is it, Gracie?" she said in a slightly relieved tone. "But what's the matter? What have you been crying about?"

"You, Lulu. Oh, I'm so sorry for you!" Gracie answered with a sob, running to her sister and putting her arms round her neck.

"Well, you needn't be. I don't care," Lulu said defiantly and with a little stamp of her foot. "No, not if all the old tyrants in the world were angry with me!"

"Oh, Lu, don't talk so!" entreated Gracie. "Do you not care if papa is displeased? Our own dear papa who loves us so dearly?"

"Yes," acknowledged Lulu, in a more quiet and subdued tone. "Oh, Gracie, why wasn't I made good like you?"

"Don't you remember the Bible verse we learned the other day?" queried Gracie. "'There is none good; no, not one.'"

"Then Grandpa Dinsmore isn't good himself and ought to have more patience with me," remarked Lulu. "But don't you fret about it, Gracie. There's no need."

"You're always sorry when I'm in trouble, and I can't help feeling so when you are," said Gracie.

Violet was dressing for dinner, thinking sadly all the while upon what she had just learned from Gracie.

"How it would trouble her father if he should hear it!" she said to herself. "I hope grandpa will not consider it necessary to report her conduct to him. Of course, according to his requirements, she should tell him herself, but I presume she will hardly have the courage to refrain from making her behavior appear less reprehensible than it actually was."

She questioned with herself whether to speak to Lulu on the subject of her misconduct, but decided not to do so at present—unless something should occur to lead to it naturally.

Her dressing completed, she went down to the parlor, and there found her grandfather alone.

He looked up with a welcoming smile—Violet had always been a particular favorite with him.

"The first down, little cricket," he said, using an old time pet name and pausing in his walk—for he was pacing the floor—to gallantly hand her to a seat on a sofa. Then, placing himself by her side, he said, "How extremely youthful you look, my dear! Who would take you for a matron?"

"To tell you a secret, grandpa," she said with a merry look, "I feel quite young still when the children are not by, and not always very old even when they are with me. By the way, how have they behaved themselves today?"

A grave, slightly annoyed, look came over his face as she asked the question.

"Max and Gracie as well as anyone could desire," he said. "But Lulu—really Vi, if she were my own child, I should try the virtue of a rod with her."

Violet's face reflected the gravity of his, while she gave vent to an audible sigh.

Mr. Dinsmore went on to describe Lulu's behavior on that and several other days. He then wound up with the question, "What do you think her father would have me do with her?"

"I suppose he would say send her to boarding school. But, grandpa, I am very loath to see that done. At the same time I cannot bear to have you annoyed with her ill-conduct, and I am thinking of attempting the task of teaching her myself."

Mr. Dinsmore shook his head. "I cannot have you annoyed with her, my little Vi—no more, at least, than you necessarily must be, occupying the relationship that you do. But we will take the matter into consideration, getting your grandma and mother to aid us with their advice."

"We won't tell her father the whole unpleasant truth, will we, grandpa?" Violet said, inquiringly and entreatingly.

"You shall tell him just what you please. I shall not trouble him in regard to the matter," Mr. Dinsmore answered in his kindliest tone.

The entrance of Mrs. Keith and Annis to the parlor put an end to the conversation, and presently dinner was announced.

Lulu obeyed the summons to the dinning room in some trepidation, not knowing what treatment to expect from Mr. Dinsmore or others who might have learned the story of her misconduct.

But there seemed no change in the manner of any of the grown people, except Mr. Dinsmore, who simply ignored her existence altogether. He was apparently unaware of her presence, never looking at her or speaking to her.

He had privately given instructions beforehand to one of the servants to attend to Miss Lulu's wants at the table, seeing that her plate was supplied with whatever viands she desired. It was done so quietly that no one even noticed anything unusual in the conduct of the meal.

Still Lulu was uncomfortably conscious of being in disgrace and seized the first opportunity to slip quietly away to her own room.

She took up the still-unfinished storybook that had begun her trouble, but could not feel the interest she had before, an uneasy conscience prevented.

Laying it aside, she sat for some moments with her elbow on the windowsill, her cheek in her hand, and her eyes gazing upon vacancy. She was thinking of what Max had said about the duty of confession to her father.

"I wish I didn't have to," she sighed to herself. "I wish papa hadn't said I must write out every day what I've been doing and send the diary to him. I think it's hard. It's bad enough to have to confess my wrong doing to him when he's at home. It's just as well he isn't, though, for I know he'd punish me if he was. Maybe he will when he comes again, but it's likely to be such a long while first that I think I'm pretty safe as far as that is concerned. Oh, it does provoke me so that he will make me obey these people! I'm determined I'll do exactly as I please when I'm grown up!

"But if I'm sent to boarding school I'll have to obey the teachers there or have a fight and be expelled. That would be an even greater disgrace and 'most break papa's heart, I do believe. They would likely be more disagreeable than even Grandpa Dinsmore—not half so nice and kind as Grandma Elsie, I'm perfectly certain. Oh dear, if I only were grown up! But I'm not, and I have to write the story of today to papa. I'll make it short."

Opening her writing desk, she took therefrom pen, ink, and paper, and, after a moment's silent cogitation, began.

"I haven't been a good girl today," she wrote. "I was so interested in a storybook that I neglected to learn my Latin lesson, so I failed in the recitation. Grandpa Dinsmore was cross and disagreeable about it. He says I answered him disrespectfully and as punishment I sha'n't go into the schoolroom or recite to him again for a week.

"There," glancing over what she had written. "I hope papa will never question me closely about it. I think he won't. It'll be such an old story by the time we meet again."

The week of her banishment from the schoolroom was an uncomfortable one for Lulu, though she was given no reason to consider herself a martyr. She was allowed a share in all the home pleasures, all her wants were as carefully attended to as usual, and she received no harsh words or unkind looks. Yet, somehow she could never rid herself of the consciousness that she was in disgrace. Very little notice was taken her by any of the family except her brother and sister. She came and went about the house as she pleased—never venturing into the schoolroom, however. But when she joined the family circle no one seemed to be aware of her presence. They talked among themselves, but did not address or even look at her.

This treatment was galling to her and she began to spend almost all of her time in "the boy's workroom" at her favorite employment of fret sawing.

Out-of-school hours Max was generally at work there also, but during those hours she had always been alone till one morning Mrs. Leland, happening to want something from a closet in the workroom, came unexpectedly upon her.

It was a surprise to both for Evelyn had kept her friend's counsel, and no one at Ion had let Elsie or anyone else for that matter into the secret of Lulu's ill conduct and consequent disgrace.

"You here, Lu?" she exclaimed on entering the room. "I heard your saw as I came up the stairway and wondered who could be busy here at this hour when the young folks are all supposed to be in the schoolroom.

"What lovely work you are doing!" she went on, drawing near to examine it. "I presume you have been extremely good and studious and so have been rewarded with leave of absence at this unusual hour. And you are certainly making good use of your holiday.

"You are wonderfully expert at this for a child of your age. Perhaps one of these days you will develop into so great a genius as to make us all proud of your acquaintance."

Lulu's cheeks burned in shame.

"You are very kind to praise my work so, Aunt Elsie," she said. "Do you really think this basket is handsome—I mean without making allowance for my age?"

"I certainly do. I think it deserves all I have said of it, if not more. How pleased your father will be when he hears what a good, industrious, and painstaking little girl he has for his eldest daughter!"

Lulu didn't speak for a moment. She was fighting a battle with herself—conscience on the one hand and love of approbation on the other were having a great struggle within her heart. She valued Mrs. Leland's good opinion and was loath to lose it.

But she was worthy of her father's glad praise, "However many and serious her faults may be, she is at least honest and truthful," and could not accept praise which she knew was wholly undeserved.

"You mistake, Aunt Elsie," she said with an effort, hanging her head in shame while her cheek flushed hotly. "I am not here for being good, but for being naughty—missing my lesson and answering Grandpa Dinsmore impertinently when he reproved me for it."

"I grieve to hear it, my dear child," Elsie returned in a truly sorrowful tone. "I had hoped you were getting quite the better of your temper and inclination to defy lawful authority. But do not be discouraged from trying again to conquer your faults. Every one of us has an evil nature and many spiritual foes to fight against. Yet, if we fight manfully, looking to Jesus for help and strength, we shall assuredly gain the victory at last, coming off more than conquerors through Him who loved us and died to save us from sin and death."

"I fear you can never think well of me again, Aunt Elsie?" Lulu said.

"I certainly hope to, Lulu," was the kind reply. "Your honest avowal is certainly to your credit. I see that you are above the meanness of falsehood and taking undeserved praise—that seems to me a very hopeful sign even as deeply ungrateful as you were toward my dear, good grandfather, who has been so kind to you and yours. Do you not think it so yourself, now that your passion has had time to cool?"

"Yes, ma'am," replied Lulu, again hanging her head and blushing. "I don't mean to behave so any more."

Then, after a moment's silence, "Aunt Elsie, I don't believe anybody has any idea how hard it is for me to be good."

"Don't you think other people find it hard, too, my poor child?" Elsie asked gently. "They also have evil natures."

"I'm sure," said Lulu, "that Max and Gracie don't have half as hard a work to be patient and sweet-tempered as I do. I often wish I'd been made good like Gracie, and I don't see why I wasn't. And there's Rosie. She doesn't ever seem to want to be willful or tempted at all to get into a passion."

"Perhaps, Lulu, she is as strongly tempted to some other sin as you are to willfulness and passion, and perhaps she falls before temptation as often. We cannot read each other's hearts. One cannot know how much another resists—as we only see the failures and not the struggles to avoid them.

"But how comforting to know that God, our heavenly Father, sees and knows it all—that He pities our weakness and proneness to sin! How precious are His promises of help in time of trial, if we look to Him for it, at the same time using all our strength in the struggle!"

"I never thought about different people having different temptations," remarked Lulu, thoughtfully. "Perhaps it isn't so much harder for me to do right than for others, after all."

"My grandfather is not unforgiving," Elsie remarked as she turned to go. "I think if you show that you are really sorry for your wrong doing, he will restore you to your former privileges."

Lulu went on with her work, but her thoughts were busy with that parting piece of advice—or rather the suggestion thrown out by Mrs. Leland.

Her pride strongly revolted against making any acknowledgment. Remembering that there was but one more day of her week left, she at length decided to await events and do the disagreeable duty only when she could no longer delay it without danger of banishment.

A remark she accidentally overheard from Rosie that afternoon made her more unwilling to apologize to Mr. Dinsmore—in fact, quite determined that she would do nothing of the kind.

Rosie was speaking to Zoe as they entered the work room together and did not notice that Lulu was there reading in a deep, window seat, where she was partially concealed by a curtain.

"I think if Lulu is wise she will soon make it up with grandpa," she was saying. "Christmas is not so very far off, and, of course, she will get nothing from him if she continues obstinate and rebellious."

Lulu did not wait to hear what Zoe might say in replay. Starting up in a fury of indignation she said, "I would have you to understand, Miss Rosie Travilla, that I am not the mercenary creature you appear to believe me. I would scorn to apologize in order to secure a gift from Mr. Dinsmore or anybody else. And if he gives me one, I shall not accept it."

"I really do not think, Lulu, you will have the opportunity to reject a gift from him," replied Rosie with what seemed to Lulu exasperating coolness. "However, I sincerely regret having said anything to rouse that fearful temper of yours. I should not have spoken so at all had I known you were within earshot."

"No, I have no doubt that you say many a mean thing of me behind my back that you would be ashamed, or afraid, to say to my face."

Rosie laughed gleefully. "Do you think I am afraid of you?" she asked in a mirthful tone, putting a strong emphasis upon the last word.

"Come, come, girls," interposed Zoe. "You surely are not going to quarrel about nothing?"

"No, I have no quarrel with anyone," replied Rosie, turning about and leaving the room with a quick, light step.

Lulu threw her book from her upon the seat from which she had just risen.

"She insults me and then walks off saying she has no quarrel with anybody!" she exclaimed passionately, addressing Zoe, who had remained behind with the laudable desire to say something to Lulu which should be as oil upon the troubled water. "It's bad enough to be abused without being forgiven for it."

"So it is," said Zoe. "But I don't think Rosie meant any harm. I sincerely believe she wants you to make it up with grandpa for your own sake—that you may have a good time now and at Christmas."

"If I can't do it from a better motive than that, I won't do it at all," said Lulu. "Aunt Zoe, I hope you have a little better opinion of me than Rosie seems to have?"

"Yes, Lulu, I've always liked you. I think yours would be a splendid character if only you could learn to rule your own spirit, as the Bible says. I've heard my father say that those who were naturally high-tempered and willful made the noblest men and women if they once thoroughly learned the lesson of self-control."

"I wish I could," said Lulu dejectedly. "I'm always sorry for my failure when my passion is over, and I think I will never indulge it again. But soon somebody does or says something very provoking, and before I have time to think of my good resolutions, I'm in a passion and saying angry words in return."

"I am sorry for you," said Zoe. "I have temper enough of my own to be able to sympathize with you. But you will try to make your peace with grandpa, won't you?"

"Not now. I was intending to, if Rosie hadn't interfered, but I sha'n't now, because if I did he would think it was from that mean motive that Rosie suggested."

"Oh, no, grandpa is too noble himself to suspect others of such meanness," asserted Zoe, defending him all the more warmly that she sometimes talked a trifle hardly of him herself.

But she saw from Lulu's stern countenance that to undo Rosie's work was quite impossible, so presently gave up the attempt and left her to solitude and her book.

CHAPTER
FOURTEENTH

How poor are they that have no patience!

— *S*HAKESPEARE

THE NEXT MORNING'S mail brought a letter from Isadore Keith to her cousin, Mrs. Elsie Travilla. It was dated "Viamede Parsonage" and written in a cheerful strain—for Isa was very happy in her married life.

She wrote rejoicingly of the prospect of seeing the Ion family at Viamede; the relatives of her husband who were now staying with them also urged an early arrival.

"We long to have you all here for the whole season," she said. "Molly and I are looking eagerly forward to your coming, and the old servants at the mansion beg for a Christmas with the family in the house. Cannot Ion spare you to Viamede this year at that season?

"I know your and uncle's kind hearts would make you both rejoice in adding to our happiness, and theirs also. And I have an additional inducement to offer. A fine school has been opened lately in the neighborhood, near enough to all our homes for our children to attend. Mine, of course, are still far to young, but I rejoice in the prospect for their future education.

"It is both a boarding and day school, principally for girls of all ages from six or eight to eighteen or twenty, but they take a few boys—typically brothers of the girls who attend.

"A gentleman and his wife are the principals, two daughters assist, and there are French and music masters as well. You will hear all about it when you come, but I am pretty certain you will find it a suitable school for all your numerous flock of children, and so uncle may take a rest from his labor of love, for such I know it has been."

The remainder of the letter was occupied with other matters not as important to this matter.

The greater part of the missive Elsie read aloud to the assembled family in the parlor, where they had gathered on leaving the breakfast table.

Then, turning to her father, she asked, "Well, papa, what do you think of it? I am rejoiced at the prospect of seeing you left to take your ease, as you surely have a right to at your age."

"Am I actually growing so extremely old?" he asked with a comically rueful look. "Really, I had flattered myself that I was still a vigorous man, capable of a great deal of exertion."

"So you seem to be, Cousin Horace," said Mr. Keith. "And certainly you are quite youthful compared to Marcia and myself."

"Oh, fie, Uncle Keith," laughed Zoe. "To insinuate that a lady is so very ancient!"

"But, my dear child, people often come, toward the close of life, to be proud of their age and perhaps sometimes to be tempted to make it appear even greater than it is."

"When they get up in the hundreds, for instance?" Edward inquired.

"Yes," said Mr. Keith with an amused smile. "Though I must not be understood as acknowledging that either my wife or myself has yet arrived at that stage."

"But we hope you will live to reach it," Elsie said with an affectionate glance from one to the other.

"Would you keep us so long from home, my sweet cousin?" Mrs. Keith asked, something in her placid face seeming to tell of longing desire to be near and like her Lord.

"Only for the sake of those to whom you are so dear, Aunt Marcia," Elsie answered, her eyes softly glistening with unshed tears.

"I shall keep them as long as ever I can," said Annis in a loving daughter tone.

There was a moment's silence, then Edward asked, "Now what about Isa's request?"

"What do you say, Elsie?" Mr. Dinsmore queried, looking at his daughter.

"That I am quite satisfied to go at whatever time will best suit the others, particularly our guests and yourself, papa."

"What do you say, Marcia?" Horace inquired of his cousin.

"That I find it delightful here and feel assured it will not be less so at Viamede, so am ready to go at once, or to stay longer, as you please."

Mrs. Dinsmore, Mr. Keith, and Annis expressed themselves in like manner.

"I think you would probably have pleasanter weather for travelling now than some weeks later in the season," remarked Edward. "And whatever else may be said of my opinion, it is at least disinterested, as I shall be the loser if you are influenced by it."

"Why, what do you mean, Ned?" asked Zoe in surprise. "Are you not going, too?"

"Not I, my dear, at least not for the winter. Business requires my presence here. I hope, though, to be able to join you all for perhaps two or three weeks over the holiday."

"I know I shall miss you sadly," he acknowledged, furtively passing his arm round her waist. As usual, they were seated side by side on a sofa. "But I know how you have been looking forward for months to this winter at Viamede, and I don't intend you shall miss it for my sake."

"But what have your intentions to do with it?" she asked with a twinkle of fun in her eye and a saucy little toss of her pretty head. "The question to be decided is what I intend, and I answer, 'Never to leave my husband, but to go when he goes and stay when he stays!' What do you say to that?"

"That I am blest with the dearest of little wives," he whispered close to her ear, tightening his clasp of her waist.

They had nearly forgotten the presence of the others, who were too busy arranging the time for setting out upon their contemplated journey to notice this bit of aside.

The children—Lulu included—were all in the room and listening with intense interest to the consultation of their elders.

At length it was settled that they would leave in a few days. Rosie, Max, Gracie, and Walter burst into exclamations of delight, but Lulu stole quietly and unobserved from the room and hurried to her own.

"Oh, I wonder," she sighed to herself as she shut the door and dropped into a chair, "if I am to go, too! I wouldn't be left behind for anything, and as there is a school there that I can be sent to as a day scholar, maybe Mamma Vi will coax to have me go. She's more likely to be in favor of taking me than anybody else—unless it's Grandma Elsie."

Just then she heard footsteps coming up the stairs, through the hall, and into the adjoining room, and the voices were of the three who were in her thoughts.

"What do you think about it, papa?" Elsie was saying. "I should be very glad to have the dear child enjoy all that the rest of us do, but it must not be at the cost of spoiling your enjoyment."

"I shall not allow it to do so," Mr. Dinsmore answered. "Lulu is a lovable child in spite of her very serious faults, and it would distress me to have her deprived of the delights of a winter at Viamede—which she has, I believe, been looking forward to with as great eagerness as any of the others, children or adults."

"I know she has, and, dear grandpa, I thank you very much for your kind willingness to take her with us," Violet responded feelingly.

Her mother added, "I also, papa. It would grieve me deeply to be compelled to leave her behind. Especially as it must necessarily be in a boarding school—Edward and Zoe being too young and inexperienced to take charge of her."

Lulu's first emotion on hearing all this was delight that she was to go. The next was gratitude to these kind friends, mingled with a deep sense of shame on account of her misconduct.

Impulsively she rose from her seat, hastened to the door of communication with the room where they were, and, pausing on the threshold, asked timidly, "Mamma Vi, may I come in?"

"Yes, Lulu," Violet answered with a kindly look and smile. And the little girl, stepping quickly to Mr. Dinsmore's side, addressed him, with eyes cast down and cheeks burning with blushes.

"I heard what you said just now, Grandpa Dinsmore, though I wasn't intending to be an eavesdropper. I thank you very much for being so kind and forgiving to me when I've been so ungrateful and troublesome to you. It makes me feel very sorry and ashamed because of my bad behavior. Will you please forgive me? I'll try to be a better girl in the future," she added with an effort.

"Surely I will, my dear child," Mr. Dinsmore responded, taking her hand and drawing her to him, then bending down to kiss her cheek and stroke her hair caressingly. "So well assured am I that you are truly sorry and desirous to do better, that I should say come back to the school room tomorrow if we were going to have lessons as usual. But as the time for setting out upon our journey to Viamede is so very near, I shall give no more lessons after today, until we return."

"Ah," glancing at his watch. "I see I should be with my pupils now." And with that he rose and left the room.

"Lulu, dear, you have made me quite happy," Elsie said, smiling affectionately upon the little girl.

"And me also," said Violet. "I know your father would feel so, too, if he were here."

"You are all so kind, you make me feel very ashamed of myself," murmured Lulu, blushing and casting down her eyes. "Mamma Vi, what can I do to help you?"

"If you would like to amuse the baby for a few minutes, that will be a help to me," Violet answered—for she saw that just now it would give Lulu sincere pleasure to think herself of use. "Her mammy is eating her breakfast," Violet continued. "And I want to speak to Christine and Alma about some sewing they are doing for me."

"I'd like to, Mamma Vi," returned Lulu, holding out her hands to little Elsie and delighting that her mute invitation was at once accepted. The sweet babe stretched out her chubby arms to her sister.

"I do think she is just as pretty and smart as she can be! Aren't you, you darling little girl?" she went on, hugging and kissing the little one with sisterly affection, while the young mother looked on with shining eyes.

It was a great relief to her that Lulu seemed to have entirely banished her former jealousy of her baby sister. That this pleasant state of affairs might continue, she was careful to make her errand to the sewing room very short, lest Lulu should begin to find her task irksome.

Hastening back to her own apartments, Violet found Lulu still in a high, good humor, laughing and romping with the little babe and allowing her to pat her cheeks and pull her dark hair with perfect impunity.

"Mamma Vi," she said, "isn't she a darling?"

"I think so," replied Violet. "But I fear she must be hurting you—for I know from experience that she can pull hair very hard."

"Oh," said Lulu, "I don't mind such a trifling hurt, as it amuses her."

Still she seemed quite ready to resign the baby to her mother.

"What more can I do, Mamma Vi?" she asked.

"Don't you want to finish that pretty bracket you were at yesterday?" asked Violet.

"Yes, ma'am, unless there is something I can do to help you."

"Nothing at present, but thank you, dear," Violet answered. Giving a parting kiss to the baby, Lulu hastened away to the workroom.

She toiled on industriously at her work, much interested in her carving—cheerful and happy. But she watched the clock on the mantel as the time drew near for Mr. Dinsmore's pupils to be dismissed from their tasks.

She had not seen Evelyn since early the day before and was longing to have a talk with her, particularly about the delightful prospect of going to Viamede to spend some months there together. And when at last the sound of child voices and laughter, coming up from below, told her that lessons were over, she sprang up and ran hastily down the stairs, looking eagerly for her friend.

She did not see Evelyn, but met Rosie face to face.

They exchanged glances—Lulu's proud and disdainful, Rosie's merry and careless—insultingly, so Lulu thought, considering what had passed between them the previous day. Drawing herself up to her full height, Lulu said, her eyes flashing with anger, "You owe me an apology!"

"Do I, indeed? Then I'm quite able to owe it," laughed Rosie, dancing away but pausing presently to throw back a parting word over her shoulder. "I'm afraid that's a very bad debt, Miss Raymond. Don't you wish you could collect it?"

Lulu's face crimsoned with anger, and she was opening her lips for a cutting retort, when Evelyn, who had just stepped out of the schoolroom, where she had lingered a moment to arrange the contents of her desk, hastily threw an arm round her waist and drew her away.

"Don't mind what Rosie says. It's really not worth caring for," she whispered. "She's full of her fun, don't you see? She doesn't mean any harm. Come, let us go up to the workroom and have a good talk."

Lulu yielded in silence, struggling hard to be mistress of herself.

Evelyn tried to help her. "Oh, Lulu, is it not delightful that we are to go so soon to that lovely Viamede?" she asked as the workroom door closed behind them.

"Yes, if only one could leave both temper and tormenting people behind!" sighed Lulu. "Oh, Eva, Rosie is so tormenting! I'd be glad to be friends with her, but she won't let me."

"It is trying," Evelyn admitted. "But you know, Lu," she went on, "that they are sent or permitted for our good—for strength grows by exercise, and if there is nothing to try our patience, how can it ever grow?"

"I have none to begin with," said Lulu.

"Oh, that's a mistake," said Evelyn. "You have great patience with your work yonder and deserve a great deal of credit for it. I do think you have much more of that kind of patience than Rosie has. But let us talk of something else."

They talked of Viamede, each telling the other what she had heard of its beauties. The talked of Magnolia Hall, too, and of Molly, Isa, and the other relatives of the Dinsmores who were living in that region of the country.

It so happened that Rosie's mother, passing through the hall below at the moment, overheard her mocking words to Lulu.

"Rosie," she called, and the little girl perceived a grieved tone in the sweet voice. "Come here, my daughter."

"Yes, mamma, dear, what is it?" Rosie asked lightly, descending the stair.

"Come into my dressing room. I want to talk to you." Then, when she was seated, "What was that I overheard you saying to Lulu just now?"

Rosie repeated her words in a careless tone.

"I desire an explanation," her mother said gently, but gravely. "What was the debt, and who owes it?"

"I, mamma, if anybody. Lulu had just said that I owed her an apology, and I had answered that if so, I was quite able to owe it."

"What had you done or said that she should think herself entitled to an apology?"

Rosie replied with a truthful account of the scene of the day before in the boys' workroom, excusing her part of it by an allusion to "Lulu's fearful temper."

"Are you quite sure, Rosie, that when you rouse it by exasperating remarks you do not share the sin?" asked her mother with a both a grieved and a troubled look.

"No, mamma, I'm afraid I do," acknowledged Rosie frankly.

"Satan is called the tempter," Elsie went on. "And I fear that you are doing his work when you willfully tempt another to sin."

"Oh, mamma," cried Rosie, looking shocked. "I never thought of that. I don't want to be his servant, doing his work. I will try never to tempt anyone to wrong-doing again."

"I am glad to hear you say that," said her mother. "And now that you are conscious of having harmed Lulu, are you not willing to do what lies in your power to repair the mischief—to pay the debt she thinks you owe her?"

Rosie's head drooped and her cheeks crimsoned. "Mamma, you are asking a hard thing of me," she said in a low, unwilling tone. "If you order me, of course, I know I must obey, but I'd rather do almost anything else than apologize to Lulu."

"I wish you to do it of your own free will and from sense of duty, not because my commands are laid upon you," Elsie answered. "Is it not the noblest course of action I am urging upon you? Is it any less mean to refuse to meet such an obligation than a moneyed one? A thing which I am sure you would be heartily ashamed to be guilty of."

"Certainly I should, mamma. One might as well steal as refuse to pay what one honestly owes, unless it be entirely out of one's power."

"You are speaking of pecuniary obligations. Now apply the same rule to this other. You have taken something from Lulu's peace of mind—a possession more valuable than money, and can you refuse an honest endeavor to restore it?"

"Mamma, you have a most convincing way of putting things," Rosie said between a smile and a sigh. "I will do as you wish and try not to repeat the offense which calls for so humiliating a reparation."

So saying, she rose and left the room, anxious to have the disagreeable duty over as soon as possible.

Rightly conjecturing Lulu's present whereabouts, she went directly to the workroom and found her and Evelyn chatting there together about their upcoming travels.

They seemed to be enjoying themselves, but a frown suddenly darkened Lulu's brow as she turned her head at the opening of the door and saw who was there.

"Excuse the interruption, girls," Rosie said quite pleasantly. "I only want to say a few words, and then I will go. Lulu, I have come to pay that debt. Mamma has convinced me that I have done very wrong in teasing you and ought to apologize. I therefore ask your pardon for any and every unpleasant word I have ever addressed to you."

Before Rosie had fairly finished what she had to say, warm-hearted, impulsive Lulu had risen to her feet, run hastily to her, and thrown her arms round her neck.

"Oh, Rosie," she cried. "I've been just too hateful for anything! I ought to be able to stand a little teasing, and you needn't apologize for vexing such a quick-tempered piece as I am."

"Yes, I should," returned Rosie. "Mamma has shown me that I have been greatly to blame. But I trust we shall be good friends after this."

"So do I," said Lulu.

CHAPTER FIFTEENTH

'Tis a goodly scene—
Yon river,
like a silvery snake, lays out
His coil i' th' sunshine,
lovingly; it breathes
Of freshness in this lap of flowery meadows.

—HUNT

"OH, ISN'T THIS SIMPLY the loveliest, loveliest country!" exclaimed Evelyn, rapturously. "What does anybody want to go to Europe for? If for beautiful scenery, I should advise them—all Americans, I mean—to travel well over their own land first."

"So should I," responded Lulu. "I don't believe there can be lovelier scenery on this earth than what we have been passing through for hours past! I wonder how near we are now to Viamede?"

"We are beside it—the estate—at this moment," remarked Mr. Dinsmore, overhearing their talk. "This orange grove is a part of it."

Exclamations of great delight followed the announcement, everybody on board the little steamer that had been threading its way up Teche Bayou and through lake and lakelet, past swamp, forest, plantation, and plain—miles upon miles of smooth, velvety lawns dotted with magnificent oaks and magnolias. Lordly villas peered through groves of orange trees. Everybody, although they had greatly enjoyed the short voyage, was glad to know they were nearing their desired haven.

A glad welcome awaited them there. As they rounded to at the little pier they could see a crowd of relatives and retainers gathered beside it, watching and waiting with faces full of joyous eagerness.

As the voyagers stepped ashore, what affectionate embraces, what glad greetings were exchanged!

Cyril and Isa Keith were there with their two little ones. Dick Percival, Bob and Betty Johnson, and—could it be possible—was that Molly Embury on her feet, standing by Mr. Embury's side and leaning only slightly on his arm?

Yes, it could be no other. Oh, wonder of wonders! She came nearer, actually walking upon the feet that no one thought would ever again be able to bear her weight.

How they gathered about her with exclamations of astonishment and delight and showered her with question upon question as to the means by which this wondrous change had been wrought!

With tears of joy and thankfulness and in tones now tremulous with deep gratitude, she and her husband told of the experiments of a rising young surgeon, which, by the blessing of God, had resulted in this astonishing cure!

"Oh, Uncle Horace, Aunt Rose, Cousin Elsie," Molly exclaimed, glancing from one to the other. "I think I am surely the happiest woman in the world, and the one who has the greatest reason for thankfulness! See, here is another precious treasure the Lord has sent me in addition to the many I had before." And turning, she beckoned to a nurse standing a little in the rear, who immediately came forward bearing an infant of only a few weeks in her arms.

"My Elsie, named for you, dear cousin," Molly said, taking the child and holding her up proudly to view. "I only hope she may, if God spares her life, grow up to be as dear and sweet and good, as kind and true and loving, as she whose name she bears."

"The darling!" Elsie said, bending down to press a kiss on the velvet cheek of her tiny namesake. "How kind of you, Molly, to name her for me! Oh, it makes me so happy to see you able to move about and with this new treasure added to your store!"

The others added their congratulations, and Mr. Embury remarked with a happy laugh, "Molly certainly thinks there was never another baby quite equal to hers in any respect."

"Which is very natural," said Mrs. Dinsmore. "I remember having some such idea about my own first baby."

The Ion children were allowed a few days of entire liberty to roam about and make themselves fully acquainted with the beauties of Viamede, Magnolia Hall, and the neighborhood before beginning school duties.

Meanwhile their elders had visited Oakdale Academy and made the acquaintance of Professor Silas Manton, his wife, and two daughters—Miss Diana and Miss Emily—who, with Signor Foresti, music master and Mr. Suarin, instructor in French, formed the corps of teachers belonging to the institution.

Privately, these friends were but indifferently pleased with any of them, but still it was decided to enter the children as pupils there for the present.

They decided to watch carefully over them and remove them at once if any evidence of harmful influence were perceived.

So far as they could learn, the parents of the pupils already there had found no cause for complaint. And, as a school was greatly needed in the vicinity, the Viamede families were desirous to aid in sustaining this should it prove, as they still hoped, a good one.

The children were naturally full of curiosity in regard to their future instructors, and gathering about the ladies on their return, plied them with questions.

"How many boys go to the school, Grandma Elsie, and who teaches them?" queried Max.

"Two questions at a time, Max!" she said pleasantly.

"Yes, ma'am, but if you will please answer one at a time I'll be entirely satisfied."

"I think the professor said there were six or eight, and he teaches them himself. That is, boys of your age and older, Max. The very little ones go into the primary department along with the little girls, and they are taught principally by Miss Emily."

"And who will teach us older girls, mamma," asked Rosie.

"Mrs. Manton hears some of the recitations; Miss Diana sits in the schoolroom all the time to keep order, and she hears most of the lessons. Professor Manton has all the classes in Latin, German, and the higher mathematics."

"Boys and girls both?" asked Lulu.

"Yes, all children are together in those studies."

"That's nice," Max said with satisfaction.

"You like the idea of going to school again, Max?"

"Oh, yes, Grandma Elsie. If the fellows I'll be put with are nice. You know I haven't had a boy companion for a long time—as a schoolmate, I mean. But if they turn out sneaks or bullies, I shall not enjoy their company. I'd rather be with the girls."

"Oh, Max, how complimentary!" cried Rosie, laughingly. "You would actually prefer our company to that of bullies and sneaks!"

"Now, Rosie, you needn't make fun of me," he said, echoing the laugh. "I didn't mean that you— that girls—were only a little to be preferred to such rakish fellows."

"How far is Oakdale Academy from here, Grandma Elsie?" asked Lulu.

"Two miles, perhaps a trifle more."

"I think I could walk it—at least in pleasant weather," remarked Evelyn.

"You will not be required to do that, my dear," said Grandma Elsie, smiling kindly upon her. "The carriage will take you all there every morning and bring you home again when school duties are over for the day."

"How nice! How very kind you are to us all!" exclaimed Evelyn. "But I think I should enjoy the walk some days with pleasant company and time enough to take it leisurely."

"Should you? Then I shall try to manage it for you. But it would not do at all for you to go entirely alone."

"If you'll just let me be her escort, Grandma Elsie, I'll walk beside her with pleasure and take the very best care of her," said Max proudly, assuming quite a manly air.

"I'd want a bigger and stronger man than you, Max," remarked Rosie teasingly.

"Then I won't offer my services to you, Rosie," he answered with dignity, while Lulu gave Rosie a displeased glance, which the latter did not seem to notice at all.

"Never mind, Max, I appreciate your offered services and shall not be afraid to trust myself to your care," Evelyn said in a lively tone. And, putting an arm affectionately round Lulu's waist, "Come, Lu, let us go out on the lawn. I saw some lovely flowers there that I want to gather for Aunt Elsie's adornment this evening."

So the little group scattered, and Gracie followed Violet to her dressing room.

"What is it, dear? Is anything wrong with my little girl?" asked Vi, noticing that the child was unusually quiet and wore a troubled look on the face that was wont to be without a cloud.

"Not much, mamma—only—only I've never been to school, and—I'm—afraid of strange people."

A sob came with the last word, and the tears began to fall.

"Then you shall not go, darling. You shall stay at home and say your little lessons to your mamma," Violet said, sitting down and drawing the little girl to her with a tender caress.

"Oh, mamma, thank you! How good you are to me!" cried Gracie, glad smiles breaking suddenly through the rain of tears, as she threw her arms round Violet's neck and held up her face for another kiss.

"But I will go if you think I ought," she added the next moment. "For you know I want to do right and please Jesus."

"Yes, dear, I know you are trying all the time to please Him. I can see it very plainly, but I shall be glad to keep my darling at home with me. And that being the case, I do not think your conscience need trouble you if you stay at home. The academy people will have no cause to complain, because you were not promised positively to them."

"Dear mamma, you've made me so happy!" exclaimed Gracie, hugging Violet with all her little strength. "I'm so obliged to papa for giving me such a dear, sweet, kind mother."

"And I am obliged to him for the dear little daughter he has given me," Violet responded with a low, pleased laugh.

Grandma Elsie sat alone on the veranda, the rest having gone away—except Max, who lingered at a little distance, now and then casting a wistful glance at her.

At length catching one of these, she gave him an encouraging smile and beckoned him to her side. "What is it, Max?" she asked. "Don't be afraid to tell me all that is in your heart."

"No, ma'am, I don't think I am—only I shouldn't like to be troublesome when you are so very kind to me—as well as to everybody else."

"I shall not think so, but I would be very glad if I can help you in any way," she answered, taking the boy's hand and looking into his eyes with so kind and motherly an expression that his heart went out to her in truly filial love.

"I hardly know just how to say it," he began with some hesitation. "But it's about the school and the new boys I'll meet there. I don't know what sort of fellows they are, and I—You know, Grandma Elsie, I'm trying so very, very hard to behave as a Christian should, and I—I'm—well, I'm afraid if they are not the right sort of boys, they—er, I might be weak enough to be led wrong as I have been before."

"Yes, dear boy, I understand you. You fear you may fall before temptation and so bring dishonor upon your profession. And doubtless so you will if you trust only in your own strength. But if, feeling that to be but weakness, you cling closely to Christ, seeking strength and wisdom from Him, He will enable you to stand.

"The apostle says, 'When I am weak, then am I strong,' and the promise is, 'God is faithful, who will not suffer you to be tempted above that ye are able, but will with the temptation also make a way to escape, that ye may be able to bear it.'"

"Thank you, Grandma Elsie. I'll try to do it," he said thoughtfully. "I'm glad that promise is in the Bible for me."

"Yes, it has often been a comfort to me," she said. "Which of His great and precious promises has not? Max, my dear boy, never be ashamed or afraid to show your colors. Stand up for Jesus always, whether at home or abroad, in the company of His friends or His foes.

"The acknowledgement that you are His follower, bound to obey His commands, may expose you to ridicule, scorn, and contempt, but if you are a good soldier of Jesus Christ, you will bear all that and more rather than deny Him."

"Oh, Grandma Elsie, could I ever do that?" he exclaimed with emotion.

"Peter did, you remember, though he had been so sure before the temptation came that he would rather die with his Master than deny Him."

"My father's son ought to be very brave," remarked Max after a moment's thoughtful silence, unconsciously thinking aloud. "I am quite sure papa would face death any time rather than desert his colors, whether for God or his country."

Elsie smiled kindly and approvingly upon the boy. It pleased her well to see how proud and fond he was of his father—how thoroughly he believed in him as the personification of all that was good and great and noble.

"I'm not nearly so brave," Max went on. "But, as papa says, the promises are mine just as much as his, and neither of us can stand except in the strength that God gives to those that look to Him for help in every hour of temptation.

"Besides, Grandma Elsie, I'll not have death to fear as Peter had. Yet I'm not sure that it isn't as hard, sometimes, to stand up against ridicule."

"Yes, I believe some do find it so. Many a man or boy has been found, in the hour of trial, so lacking in true moral courage—which is courage of the highest kind—as to choose to throw away his own life or that of another rather than risk being jeered at as a coward. Ah, Max, I hope you will always be brave enough to do right even at the risk of being deemed a coward by such as 'love the praise of men more than the praise of God.'"

"Oh, I hope so!" he returned. "And if I don't, I think there should be no excuse made for me—a boy with such a father and such friends as you and all the rest of the folks here."

"I am very pleased that you so appreciate your opportunities, Max," Elsie said.

Just at that moment Evelyn and Lulu came up the veranda steps with their hands filled with an abundance of wildflowers culled from among the myriad of beautiful ones that spangled the velvety lawn where they had been strolling together ever since leaving the house.

"See what lovely flowers, Grandma Elsie!" cried Lulu. "Oh, thank you for bringing me here to Viamede, and for saying that I may gather as many of these as I please!"

"I am very glad you enjoy it, dear child," Elsie answered. "It was one of my great pleasures as a child and is such to this day."

"I gathered mine for you and Mamma Vi," said Lulu. "And—oh, I should like to put this lovely white one in your hair, if you don't mind, Grandma Elsie," she added with a wistful look into the sweet face still so smooth and fair, in spite of the quickly passing years.

"If I don't mind? I shall be pleased to have it there," was the smiling reply. And Lulu hastened to avail herself of the gracious permission. Then, stepping back to note the effect, "Oh," she cried. "How lovely it does look against your beautiful, golden-brown hair, Grandma Elsie! Don't you think so, too, Evelyn?"

"Yes, indeed!" exclaimed both Max and Evelyn, the latter adding, "I never saw more beautiful or abundant hair or lovelier complexion. It seems really absurd to call a lady 'grandma' who looks so young."

"So it does," said Max. "But we all love her so that we want to be some relation, and we can't bear to say Mrs. Travilla. So, what else can be done about it?"

As he spoke, Gracie came running out and joined them, wearing a very bright, happy face.

"Oh, Grandma Elsie and everybody, I'm just as glad as I can be!" she cried. "I don't have to go to school, because mamma is so kind. She says she will teach me at home."

While the others were expressing their sympathy in her happiness, Mr. Dinsmore joined them.

"Here are letters," he said. "For you, Elsie, from Edward and your college boys, and one for each of the Raymonds from the captain."

He distributed them as he spoke, giving Violet's to Max with a request that he would carry it to her.

"Thank you, sir. I'll be delighted to do the errand, because nothing pleases Mamma Vi so much as a letter from papa, unless it is a sight of his face," said Max, hurrying away with it.

Gracie, always eager to share every joy with "her dear mamma," ran after him with her own letter in her hand.

What a treasure it was! A letter from papa, with her name on it in his writing, so that there could be no doubt that it was entirely her very own! How nice to have it so! But unless there was a secret in it, mamma should have the pleasure of reading it—Max and Lulu, too, for there was very little selfishness in little Gracie's sweet nature.

Lulu's face was full of gladness as she took her letter from Mr. Dinsmore's hand and, glancing at the address, recognized the well-known and loved handwriting.

"Dear Lu, I'm so very glad for you!" murmured Evelyn close to her ear, turning and walking swiftly away.

"Oh, poor, dear Evelyn! She can never get a letter from her father," thought Lulu with a deep feeling of compassion, as she sent one quick glance after the retreating figure.

But her thoughts instantly returned to her treasure, and she hurried to the privacy of her own room to enjoy its perusal unobserved.

Reading what her father had written directly to her, and her alone, was like having a private interview with him. Besides, he might have said something that would touch her feelings, and she could not bear to have any of "these people" see her cry.

It was not a long letter, but tenderly affectionate. He called her his dear child, his darling little daughter, and told her he was very often thinking of and praying for her—asking that God would bless her in time and eternity, that He would help her to conquer her faults and grow up to good and useful womanhood, and that when her life on earth was done He would receive her to glory and immortality in the better land.

He spoke of having received flattering accounts of her studiousness and general good behavior since last he parted from her, and he said that until she should become a parent herself she could never know the joy of heart it had given him. He knew that she must have fought many a hard battle with her besetting sins, and while he hoped that a desire to please God had been among her motives, he rejoiced in believing that love for him had also influenced her.

"And it makes me very happy to think so, my precious little daughter. I am very glad to be able to bestow praise upon you rather than reproof," he added.

Lulu's cheeks grew hot with shame as she read these words of commendation—now so undeserved—and tears started to her eyes as, in her own imagination, she saw the look of deep pain and distress that would come over her father's face when he learned of her late misconduct.

"Oh, why am I not a better girl?" she sighed to herself. "How could I behave so when I know it grieves my dear papa like that?"

CHAPTER SIXTEENTH

Lulu's Protest

LULU'S SELF-UPBRAIDING was broken in upon by a gentle tap at her door followed by Gracie's voice saying in glad, eager tones, "Come, Lulu, mamma is going to read us some of her letter from papa. And you shall see mine, too, if you want to."

"Yes, I'll be there in a minute," Lulu replied, and jumping up and hastily folding her letter, she slipped it into its envelope, and that into her pocket.

This done, she hurried into Violet's dressing room and joined Max and Gracie as listeners to the reading of her father's letter to his wife.

At its conclusion Max offered the one he had received, saying, "Now please read mine aloud, Mamma Vi. I'm sure you would all like to hear it."

"Mine, too," Gracie said, laying hers in Violet's lap.

When these had been read, both Max and Gracie turned expectantly to Lulu.

"Mine is just a nice, little talk meant only for me," she said.

"Then, dear, we won't ask to see it," Violet answered pleasantly, and the others seemed satisfied with the explanation.

"Papa hasn't heard about the school. I wonder what he would think," remarked Lulu.

"I have no doubt he would approve of anything done for you by my mother and grandfather," Violet answered gently.

"When do we begin there?" asked Max.

"Next Monday. But you are to be taken over this afternoon for a preliminary examination, so that you may be assigned your places and lessons and be ready to set to work with the other students on Monday morning.

"Will you go with us, Mamma Vi?" asked Lulu.

"No, dear, but mamma and grandpa will."

"I must go and tell Eva, so she will be ready, too," exclaimed Lulu, starting up and hurrying from the room.

Evelyn had wandered to a distant part of the grounds and seated herself upon a little, grassy mound that encircled the roots of a great oak tree.

With the sight of Lulu's joy at receiving a letter from her absent father a fresh sense of her own heavy bereavement had come over her, and her heart seemed breaking with its load of bitter sorrow—its intense longing for, "the touch of a vanished hand; and the sound of a voice that is still!"

She sat with her hands clasped in her lap and her eyes gazing far out over the bayou, while tears coursed freely down her cheeks and her bosom heaved with sobs.

It was her habit to go away and weep in solitude when calmness and cheerfulness seemed no longer within her power.

Presently a light step approached, but she did not hear it. She deemed herself still alone till someone sat down beside her and passed an arm round her waist, tenderly kissing her forehead.

"Dear child," said her Aunt Elsie's sweet voice, "do not grieve so. Think how blest he is—forever freed from all earth's cares and troubles, pains and sicknesses, and forever with the Lord he loved so well."

"Yes, oh, I am glad for him!" she cried. "But how, oh, how shall I learn to live without him?"

"By getting nearer to Him who has said, 'I will be a Father of the fatherless; I will never leave thee, nor forsake thee.'

"Dear child, Jesus loves you with a purer, deeper, stronger love than any earthly parent can feel for his child.

"And He will not allow any trial to visit you which shall not be for your good. He will give you strength to bear all that He appoints, and when the work of grace is done will take you to be forever with Himself and the dear ones gone before."

"Yes, Aunt Elsie, thank you. It is very sweet and comforting to know and remember all that—and He has given me such a good home with both you and uncle, and everybody is so kind to me. I ought to be happy. I am most of the time, but now and then such a longing for papa comes over me that I am compelled to go away by myself and indulge my grief for a little. Do you think it is wrong to do so?"

"No, dear. Jesus wept at the grave of Lazarus, and He did not rebuke the sisters for indulging their grief, so I cannot believe our kind heavenly Father would forbid us the relief of tears."

The conversation gradually drifted to other themes, and when Lulu joined them there under the tree, they were talking of the studies Evelyn should pursue at Oakdale.

Lulu made her communication, then she and Evelyn went into the house to dress for dinner and the drive which was to be taken immediately after.

Each rejoiced that they were to be together in this new experience, and they were greatly pleased when, having examined them in their studies, Professor Manton assigned them to the same classes and to adjoining desks.

They were pleased, too, with Oakdale. It had been a very fine place before the war—the residence of a family of wealth and standing. Now, though, in a measure fallen into decay, it was still an attractive spot—not destitute of beauty.

The rooms appointed to study and recitation were of good size, airy, well lit, and with a pleasant outlook—here upon lawn and lakelet, there on a garden, shrubbery, or orange grove.

"I think it is a beautiful place for a school," Lulu remarked as they were on their homeward way. "We shall enjoy wandering about the grounds or sitting under the trees on the lawn at recess."

"Or having a game of ball," said Max.

"Do you like Professor Manton, Eva?" asked Lulu with a look of disgust as she mentioned his name.

"I don't know him yet," Evelyn replied, smiling. "I intend to try to like him."

"I don't!" cried Lulu with vehemence. "He's pompous and too—what is it?"

"Fawning," supplied Max. "I'm just certain he has heard that Grandpa Dinsmore and Grandma Elsie are very rich, and I guess he thinks we are their own grandchildren."

"Perhaps it is just as well, if it will make him treat you all the better," remarked Rosie. "Therefore, I shall not enlighten him. I have formed the same opinion of him that you and Lulu have, Max."

"But don't let us judge him too hastily," said Evelyn. "Thinking ill of him will only make it hard to treat him with the respect we should while we are his pupils."

"Very sage advice, Miss Leland," laughed Rosie. "But seriously, I am sure you are quite right."

"So am I," said Max. "And I, for one, intend to try to behave and study exactly as if he were as worthy of respect as even Grandpa Dinsmore himself."

"I, too," said Evelyn. "As if all the teachers were."

"Very good resolutions," said Rosie. "So I adopt them myself."

"Well," sighed Lulu, "resolutions don't seem to amount to much with me, but I haven't the least intention of misbehaving or wasting my time and the boundless opportunities."

She said it earnestly, really meaning every word of it.

The children would probably not have expressed themselves quite so freely in the presence of their elders, but they were alone in the carriage—Mr. Dinsmore and his daughter having prepared to take the trip on horseback.

Rosie, however, reported to her mother that part of the conversation relating to their intended good conduct, and so greatly rejoiced her heart. She had been somewhat anxious in regard to the impression made upon the children—especially Lulu, who was a keen observer of character—by the professor, and its effect upon their behavior toward him. She had feared that Lulu, who never did anything by halves, would conceive a great contempt and dislike for the man, in which case there would be small hope of her conducting herself at all as she should while attending the school.

Mr. Dinsmore and Violet had shared her fears, and they consulted together as to the measures it might be wise to take in hope of averting the unpleasant and trying occurrences which they feared.

"Do you think I should talk with her about it?" asked Violet. "Oh, if only I knew what it would be best to say!"

"Perhaps the less the better," her grandfather said with a smile. "I should advise you not to prepare a set sermon, but to say nothing unless upon the spur of the moment, when something she does or says may lead naturally to it."

"No, do not let us disgust her with long lectures," said Elsie. "She is a child that will not endure a great deal in the way of reproof or admonition.

"But perhaps, papa, a few words from you, who are certainly much wiser than either Vi or myself, might have a good effect."

"No," he said. "She respects you quite as much as she does me and loves you far better. You are the one whose words will be most likely to benefit her."

"Then I will undertake it, asking for wisdom from above that I may do her good and not harm," Elsie replied in a low, earnest tone.

The task thus devolving upon her, she seized a suitable moment when alone with Lulu to remind her that she now had an opportunity to establish a character for diligence and good behavior, as she was taking a new start among strangers. Home friends, too, were quite ready to believe that she had turned over a new leaf and would henceforth strive to be and to do just what would please her heavenly Father and the dear earthly one who loved her so fondly.

The words were accompanied by a tender caress, and Lulu, looking up brightly, lovingly into the kind face bending over her, impulsively threw her arms round Elsie's neck, saying, "Yes, indeed, dear Grandma Elsie, I do mean to try with all my might to be a good girl and to learn all I possibly can.

"I am not at all sure of success, though," she added, her face clouding over and her eyes seeking the floor.

"Dear child," Elsie said, "remember that the Lord says to us, 'In Me is thine help.' Look to Him for help and strength in every time of trial, and you will come off at last more than conqueror."

"How kind you are, Grandma Elsie!" Lulu said gratefully. "I think you do believe in me yet— believe that I do really want to be good, though I have failed so often."

"My dear little girl, I have not a doubt of it," was the kind response. Lulu's heart grew light. The trustful words gave her renewed hope and courage for the fight with her besetting sins.

And she, along with the others made a very fair beginning, winning golden opinions from their teachers and peers.

Both Max and the girls found pleasant companions among their new schoolmates, while they found the principal of the institution less disagreeable than they had at first esteemed him. They all agreed, though, among themselves that it would be quite impossible ever to feel any affection for him, his wife, or Miss Diana, with whom the little girls had most to do.

They all liked Miss Emily best, but Walter was the only one of the number belonging to her department, and she seldom came into direct contact with any of the others.

They all took lessons in French, and as Signor Foresti had the reputation of being a very fine music teacher, it had been arranged that the three little girls should be numbered among his pupils. But the first day, Lulu, on coming home from school, went to Violet with a strong protest against being taught by him.

"Mamma Vi," she said, "the girls in his class say he has a dreadful, dreadful temper, gets angry and abusive when they make the slightest mistake, and sometimes strikes them with a whalebone pointer he always has in his hand. That is, he snaps it on their fingers, and it hurts terribly. I shouldn't mind the pain so much, but it would just make me furious to be disgraced by a blow from anybody, especially a man—unless it were papa, who would have a right, of course," she added with a blush. "So, Mamma Vi, please save me from having him for my teacher."

Violet looked much perplexed and disturbed. "Lulu, dear, it doesn't rest with me to decide the matter, you know," she said in a soothing, sympathetic tone. "If it did, I should at once say you need not. But I will speak to grandpa and mamma about it."

"Well, Mamma Vi, if I must try it, won't you tell him beforehand that he is never to strike me? If he does, I'll not be able to restrain myself, and I'll strike him back. I just know I shall. And then we'll all be sorry I was forced to take lessons from him."

"Lulu, my dear child, I hope you would never do that!" cried Violet in distress. "How would your father feel? What would he say when he heard of it?"

"I don't know, Mamma Vi, but I don't believe he would allow that man to strike me, and I dare say he would think it served him right if I strike him back. However, I don't mean to be understood as having formed the deliberate purpose to do so—only I feel that that's what I should do without waiting a second to think."

Violet thought it altogether likely and after a moment's cogitation promised that the signor should be told that he could have Lulu for a pupil only with the distinct understanding that he was never, on any account, to give her a blow.

"But, Lulu, dear," she added entreatingly, "you will try not to furnish him the slightest excuse for punishing you, will you?"

"No, Mamma Vi, but I do want to escape taking lessons from him—for fear we might fall out and have a fight," returned the little girl, laughing to keep from showing that she was almost ready to cry with vexation at the very idea of being compelled to become a pupil of the fiery, little Italian.

He was a diminutive man of forbidding aspect.

"I fear that in that case you would get the worst of it," Violet remarked with a faint smile.

"He is only a little man, Mamma Vi," Lulu said, shaking her head in dissent. "The professor would make two of him, I think."

"And you are only a little girl, and men and boys are, as a rule, far stronger than women and girls," replied Violet. "But aside from that consideration, it would be a dreadful thing for you to come to a collision, and I shall certainly do what I can to prevent it."

In pursuance of that end she presently went in search of her mother and grandfather.

She found them and Mrs. Dinsmore seated together on the lawn. The ladies were busied with their needlework, and Mr. Dinsmore was reading aloud.

As Violet approached, he paused and laid the open book down on his knee, making room for her by his side.

"Don't let me interrupt you, grandpa," she said, accepting his mute invitation.

"Perhaps grandpa is ready to rest," remarked her mother. "He has been reading steadily for more than an hour."

"Yes, I am ready to hear what my little cricket has to say," he said, looking inquiringly at Violet.

"It will keep, grandpa," she answered lightly.

"No," he said. "Let us have it now. I see that something is causing you anxiety, and you have come to ask counsel or help in some direction."

"Ah, grandpa," she responded with a smile, "you were always good at reading faces." Then she went on to repeat the conversation just held with Lulu.

"What do you say, grandpa, grandma, and mamma?" she wound up. "Shall we insist on her taking music lessons from Signor Foresti?"

"Yes," said Mr. Dinsmore with decision. "He is an uncommonly fine teacher, and it is desirable that she should enjoy, or rather profit by, his instructions. Also, it is high time she should become thoroughly convinced of the necessity of controlling that violent temper of hers. She needs to be taught submission to lawful authority, too, and indulging her in this whim would, in my judgment, be likely to have a very opposite effect. What do you say, Rose and Elsie?"

"I presume you are right, Horace, as you usually are," replied his wife.

"I prefer to leave the question entirely to your decision, papa," said Elsie. "But shall we not yield to the child's wishes as far as to warn the man beforehand that he is never, upon any pretext, to give her a blow? I will not have him strike Rosie," she added with heightened color. "If he ventured such a thing I should take her immediately away."

Her father regarded her with an amused smile. "I have seldom seen you so excited, so nearly angry, as at that thought," he remarked. "But Rosie is not at all likely to give him any pretext for so doing, nor is Evelyn. They are both remarkably even-tempered and painstaking with their studies.

"However, I shall warn Signor Foresti in regard to his treatment of all three of the little girls sent by us to the school, telling him that if they are idle or wanting in docility and respect he is simply to report them for discipline at home. Will that answer, Violet?"

"Nicely, thank you, grandpa," she said with a sigh of relief.

Lulu looked only half satisfied when her mamma reported the result of her intercession with those higher in authority than she. But, seeing there was nothing more to be gained, she quietly submitted to the inevitable.

CHAPTER
SEVENTEENTH

The Collision

IT WAS A BLESSING TO Lulu at this time that she had such a friend as Evelyn Leland constantly at her side in the schoolroom and on the playground. Their mutual affection grew and strengthened day by day. Eva was most anxious to be a true and helpful friend to her dear Lulu. How could she better prove herself such than by assisting her to conquer in the fight with her fiery temper which had so often got her in sore trouble?

Evelyn set herself earnestly to the task, urging Lulu to renewed efforts. She encouraged her after every failure with assurances of final victory if she would but persevere in the conflict. She was also ever on the watch to warn her of threatening danger.

If she did see anger begin to flash from Lulu's eye or deepen the color on her cheek, she would remind her of her good resolutions by an entreating look or a gentle touch or pressure of her hand.

She thus warded off many an outburst of passion, and Lulu, like the others, was able each week to carry home a good report of conduct—of lessons, also—for she was much interested in her studies, very ambitious to excel, and therefore both very industrious and painstaking.

All went well for the five or six weeks between their entrance into Oakdale and the Christmas holidays.

The older people were careful to make that holiday week a merry time for the children. Each one received numerous beautiful gifts, and visits were exchanged with the families of Magnolia Hall and the parsonage.

Scarcely ever a day passed in which there was not some exchange between the three families, but at this holiday time there were special invitations and more than ordinary activity.

Then, the holidays over, it was a little difficult to settle down again to work and study. The children, and probably the teachers also, found it so. However that may have been, there was certainly more than the usual friction in the working of the school machinery. The teachers reproached the scholars with want of attention and lack of industry, and the latter grumbled to each other that the professor and Miss Diana snubbed them, and Mrs. Manton and the French teacher wasted neither patience nor politeness upon them.

Also, those whose turn it was to take a music lesson reported Signor Foresti just as unbearable, testy and faultfinding.

Fortunately, Lulu was not of the number, but her respite was only for a day. Her heart sank as she thought of the danger of a collision between him and herself.

She thoroughly disliked him but hitherto had been able to control herself and avoid any clashing of her temper with his. It had not always been an easy thing for her to do, he having bestowed upon her many a sharp word that she had felt to be altogether undeserved.

She gave herself great credit for her continued forbearance and thought she could not reasonably be expected to exercise it much longer. Yet she knew that failure would entail dire consequences.

Evelyn knew all about her trials and trembled for her friend.

"Oh, Lu," she said, when they found themselves alone together at home on the evening of that first day after their return to school duties. "Do let us make up our minds to bear and forbear tomorrow when we take our music lessons and not give Signor Foresti the pleasure of seeing that we care for his crossness."

"Indeed!" cried Lulu. "I've put up with enough of it, and I'll be apt to tell him so if he's much worse than usual."

"Oh, Lu, don't!" entreated Evelyn. "You have borne so splendidly with him, and what a pity it would be to spoil it now by giving in to impatience!"

"Yes, but I can't bear everything. I'm astonished at myself for having put up with so much. I don't believe I could have if it hadn't been for your help, Eva."

"I'm very glad if I have been any assistance to you in keeping your temper, dear Lulu," Evelyn answered with a look of pleasure. "And oh, I should so like to help you to go on as you have already begun."

"Well, if I don't it will be his fault. It would take the patience of a saint to bear forever with his injustice and ill temper. I know I have a bad temper, but I'm sure his is a great deal worse."

"I do really think it is, Lu. But other people having worse faults doesn't make ours any better. Besides, do you suppose he has had good religious teaching as you and I have?"

"No, of course not. But I never thought of that before. He's a man, though, and a man ought to be expected to have better control of himself than a little girl."

Evelyn and Lulu took their music lessons on the same day of the week—Evelyn first, then Lulu immediately after.

They met the next day at the door of the music room, the one coming out and the other just about to enter.

Evelyn was looking pale and agitated, and Lulu was flushed and angry, having been scolded—unjustly she thought—by Miss Diana, who accused her of slighting a drawing with which she had really taken great pains.

"Oh, Lu, do be careful—the slightest mistake angers him today," whispered Evelyn in passing.

"It always does," said Lulu gloomily.

"But you will be on your guard?" Lulu nodded in assent and stepped into the room with a "Good morning, signor."

"Good morning, mees. You are von leetle moment too late."

Deigning no reply, Lulu took possession of the piano stool, spread out her music, and began to play.

"Dat ish too fast, mees. You should not make it like a gallop or a valtz," stormed the little man.

Without a word Lulu changed her time, playing very slowly.

"Now you make von funeral dirge," he cried fiercely. "Play in de true time or I vil—"

"You will what?" she asked coolly, as he paused without finishing his sentence.

"Report you, mees."

She merely flashed a scornful glance at him out of her great, dark eyes and went on with her exercise, really doing her best to play it correctly.

But nothing would please him. He continued to fume and scold till he succeeded in confusing the child so that she blundered sadly.

"You are striking false notes, mees!" he roared. "I will not have it!" And with the words a stinging blow from his pointer fell across the fingers of her left hand.

Instantly Lulu was on her feet, white with concentrated passion. The next she had seized the music book in both hands and dealt the cowardly assailant a blow with it on the side of his head and face that nearly stunned him and gave him a black eye for a week.

At the same moment the piano stool came down upon the floor with a crash, upset by her whirling round to reach him. Before he knew what had happened, she was out of the room, slamming the door behind her.

Never had she been in a greater fury of passion. She rushed out into the grounds and paced rapidly to and fro for several minutes, trying to regain sufficient calmness to dare venture back into the schoolroom—not caring to appear there either for some minutes, as the hour for her music lesson had not yet fully expired.

When she thought it had, she went quietly in and took her accustomed seat.

Miss Diana was busy with a recitation and took no notice, but Evelyn, glancing at Lulu's flushed face and sparkling eyes, perceived at once that something was wrong with her.

The rules of the school forbade questioning her then. She could only wait until they should be dismissed.

Another pupil had gone to Signor Foresti a moment before Lulu's entrance into the schoolroom.

When her hour had expired she came back with a face full of excitement and curiosity. She glanced eagerly, inquiringly at Lulu, then turning to Miss Diana said, "Signor Foresti says Miss Raymond did not finish her lesson, and he wishes her to come back and do it now."

"Singular!" remarked Miss Diana, elevating her eyebrows. "Do you hear, Miss Raymond? You can go."

"I do not wish to go, Miss Diana," replied Lulu, steadying her voice with some difficulty.

"Indeed! That has nothing to do with it, and you will please go at once."

Lulu sat still in her seat with a look of stubborn determination on her face.

"Do you hear, Miss Raymond?" asked the teacher, raising her voice to a higher key.

"Yes, ma'am, but I shall never take another lesson from that man."

"And why not, pray?"

"Because he is not a gentleman."

Miss Diana looked utterly astonished. "Well, really!" she exclaimed at length. "I shall not discuss that point with you at present, but it has nothing to do with the matter at hand. Will you be pleased to go and finish your music lesson?"

"No, ma'am. I have said I shall never be taught by him again, and I am not one to break my word," concluded Lulu.

"Very well, miss, we shall see what my father has to say to that."

She stepped to the door and summoned him.

He came, marching in with his most pompous air, and glanced around, inquiring what was wanted.

A great hush had fallen on the room. There was not a whisper, not a movement—eyes and ears were intent upon seeing and hearing all that should pass.

Miss Diana, glancing from her father to Lulu, drew herself up haughtily and replied, "Miss Raymond refuses obedience to orders."

"Indeed!" he said, his frown growing darker and expending itself entirely upon the culprit. "How is that? What were the orders, and what reason does she assign for refusing obedience?"

"The signor sent word that she had not finished her music lesson, and that he desired her to return and do so. I directed her to obey the summons, and she flatly refused—giving as her only reason that he was not a gentleman."

"Not a gentleman!" repeated the professor in accents of astonishment and indignation. "Not a gentleman! In making such an assertion, young miss, you insult not the signor merely, but myself also, since it was I who engaged him to give instruction in music to the pupils of this establishment. Pray, miss, on what do you found your most absurd opinion?"

"Upon his conduct, sir," replied Lulu, returning the man's stare undauntedly as her cheeks reddened and her eyes flashed with anger. "He has treated me today as no gentleman would ever treat a lady or a little girl."

"How?"

"Scolding and storming when I was doing my very best and going on to actually strike me—me who he was forbidden from the very first ever to strike. Both Grandpa Dinsmore and Grandma Elsie—I mean Mrs. Travilla—forbade it when they put me in his class, for I had told them I wouldn't be taught by him if he was allowed to treat me so, and they said he should not."

"Ah! He should not have done so. I do not allow girls to be punished in that manner here. I shall speak to the signor about it. But you will go and finish your lesson."

Lulu made no movement to obey and made no reply except a look that said plainly that she had no intention of obeying.

"Did you hear me, miss?" he asked wrathfully.

"I did, but I have already said several times that I would never be taught by that man again."

He made a step toward her and a threatening gesture, but paused, seeming to consider a moment, then said, "We will see what your guardians have to say about that." He turned and left the room.

Everyone seemed to draw a long breath of relief, and smiles, nods, and significant glances were excitedly exchanged.

"The hour for the closing of school has arrived, young ladies, and you are dismissed," said Miss Diana, and she sailed from the room.

Instantly the girls, some twenty in number, flocked about Lulu with eager exclamations and questions.

"Did he really strike you, Lu?"

"How did you take it?"

"I hope you returned the blow? I certainly shall if ever he dares to lift his hand to me." This came from a brunette of fourteen or fifteen.

"Brings it down, you mean, with a snap of his pointer on your fingers," laughed a merry little girl with golden hair and big, blue eyes.

Neither Rosie nor Evelyn had spoken as yet, though the one was standing and the other sitting close at Lulu's side.

Lulu's left hand lay in her lap with her handkerchief wrapped loosely about it. Eva gently removed the handkerchief and tears sprang to her eyes at the sight of the wounded fingers.

"Oh, Lu!" she cried in accents of love and pity. "How he has hurt you!"

A shower of exclamations followed from the others. "Hasn't he? The vile wretch!"

"Cruel monster! Worst of savages! He ought to be flogged within an inch of his life!"

"He ought to be shot down like a dog!"

"He ought to be hung!"

"It's a very great shame," said Rosie, putting her arm affectionately round Lulu's neck. "I hope grandpa will have him arrested and sent to prison."

"But, Lu," cried Nettie Vance, the one who had brought the signor's message. "Do tell me, did you not strike him back? He looked as if he had had a pretty heavy blow on the side of his face."

"So he had—as hard a one as I could give with the music book in both hands," replied Lulu, smiling grimly at the recollection.

Her statement was received with great peals of laughter, clapping of hands, and cries of, "Good for you, Miss Raymond!"

"Oh, but I'm glad he got his deserts for once!"

"I think he'll be apt to keep his hands—or rather his pointer—off you in the future."

"Off other people, too," added a timid little girl who had felt its sting more than once. "I was rejoiced to hear the professor say he didn't allow such punishment for girls. I'll let the signor know, and I'll inform on him if ever he touches me with his pointer again."

"So should I," said Nettie. "I wouldn't put up with it. But he has never hurt you as he has Lulu. See! Every one of her fingers is blistered!"

"Yes, it must have hurt terribly. I don't wonder she struck him back."

"Indeed, it wasn't the pain I cared so much for," returned Lulu, scorning the implication. "It was the insult."

"Young ladies," said a severely reproving voice behind them, "why are you tarrying here? It is high time you were all on your homeward way. Miss Rosie Travilla, Miss Evelyn Leland, and Miss Raymond, the Viamede carriage has been waiting for the last half hour."

The speaker was no other than Mrs. Manton who had entered unperceived by them in their excitement.

No one replied to her rebuke, but there was a sudden scurrying into the cloakroom, followed by a hasty donning of hats and wraps.

Rosie brought up the rear, muttering as she drew out and glanced at a pretty, little watch, "Hardly so long as that, I am sure!"

"Ah, you can't expect perfect accuracy under such trying circumstances," laughed Nettie Vance.

"Wait, Lu," said Evelyn softly. "Let me help you with your cloak or you will be sure to hurt those poor fingers."

"How kind you are, Eva!" whispered Lulu, her face lighting up with pleasure as she accepted the offer. "How good you are to me! Oh, it is nice to have such a friend as you!"

CHAPTER

EIGHTEENTH

For what I will, I will, and there's an end.

—SHAKESPEARE

Max WAS ON THE veranda waiting, like the gentleman that he was, to hand the girls into the carriage.

Hardly were they seated therein and the door closed upon them, when he exclaimed, "Why, what's the matter?"

"Why do you think anything is?" queried Rosie with an attempt to laugh.

"Because you all look so excited, and—what's your hand wrapped up for, Lu?"

She removed the handkerchief and held the hand out before him.

"Who did that? Who dared do such a thing to my sister?" he asked hotly, his face crimsoning with anger and indignation.

"Never mind who," said Lulu.

"Signor Foresti," said Rosie. "I hope grandpa will have him fired and imprisoned for it—such a cowardly, savage attack as it was!"

"I only wish I was big enough and strong enough to flog him well for it," growled Max, clenching his fists and speaking between his shut teeth. "If papa were here, I think the cowardly villain wouldn't escape without a sound drubbing."

Lulu laughed rather hysterically as she said, "I took the law into my own hands, Max, and I punished him pretty well for it, I believe."

"You did!" he exclaimed in utter astonishment. "How? I shouldn't think you had the strength to grapple with him."

"I didn't, exactly, but before he knew what was coming, I hit him a blow that I think nearly knocked him down," and she went on to repeat the whole story for Max's benefit.

The occurrence was the theme of conversation all the way home, and on their arrival, Mr. Dinsmore and the ladies being found on the veranda, the case was at once laid before them in all its details.

All were indignant at the treatment Lulu had received, but also shocked at her retaliation.

"You should not have done that," Mr. Dinsmore said reprovingly. "It was by no means ladylike. I should not have blamed you for at once vacating the piano stool and walking out of the room, but his punishment should have been left to older and wiser hands."

"There's enough more owing him for older and wiser hands to attend to," remarked Lulu. "And I hope it won't be neglected."

An amused smile trembled about the corners of Mr. Dinsmore's mouth, but only for an instant.

"Measures shall be taken to prevent a recurrence of the unpleasantness of today," he said with becoming gravity. "I shall myself call upon the signor and warn him to beware of ever repeating it upon anyone."

"He won't repeat it to me, because I shall never take another lesson from him," said Lulu, steadily and looking straight into Mr. Dinsmore's eyes as she spoke.

"The choice is not with you," he answered a little sternly. "You are under orders and must do as you are bid. But we will not discuss the matter further at present," he added with a wave of the hand, as if dismissing her.

She turned to go—in no very amiable mood.

"Lulu, dear," said Grandma Elsie, rising and following her. "Those poor fingers must be attended to. I have some salve which will be soothing and healing to them. Will you come with me and let me dress them with it?"

"Yes, ma'am, thank you," the child answered half chokingly, the kind sympathy expressed in the words and tones quite overcoming her with a strong reaction from the stubborn, defiant mood into which Mr. Dinsmore's closing remarks had thrown her.

Mr. Dinsmore's decision was a disappointment to all the children. For once, even Rosie was inclined to warmly espouse Lulu's cause. Though standing in considerable awe of her grandfather, she ventured upon a mild remonstrance.

"Grandpa, don't you think that man has behaved badly enough to deserve to lose his pupil?"

"I do most decidedly," he answered. "But Lulu is improving wonderfully under his tutelage, and should not, I think, be allowed to lose the advantage of it while we remain here."

"I very much fear his usefulness is over so far as she is concerned," sighed Violet. "And, grandpa, I dread the struggle you will certainly have with her if you insist upon her continuance of his class. I never saw a more determined look than the one she wore when she said that she would never take another lesson from him."

"Do not trouble yourself," he said. "I think I am fully equal to the contest. I should gladly avoid it if it seemed to me right to do so, but it does not. It is high time Lulu was taught proper submission to lawful authority."

Max, standing with averted face, a little apart from the speaker, heard every word that was said.

The boy was sorely troubled. He turned and walked away, saying to himself, "She will never do it. I don't believe any power on earth can make her. And Grandpa Dinsmore is about as determined as she, so what is to come of it I can't tell. Oh, if papa were only here! Nobody else can manage Lu when she gets into one of her stubborn fits, and I don't believe he'd make her go back to that horrid savage of a music teacher. I've a notion to write and tell him all about it. But no, where would be the use? I dare say the whole affair will be over before my letter could reach him and an answer come back."

Very tenderly and carefully Elsie bound up the wounded fingers. Then, taking the little girl in her arms, she kissed her kindly, saying, "You were treated very badly, my dear child, and it is not likely the man will venture to act so again after my father has spoken to him and warned him of the consequences of such behavior."

"I think he won't to me," Lulu answered—the stubborn, defiant look returning to her face.

"Do the fingers feel better?" Elsie asked gently.

"Yes, ma'am, and I am very much obliged. Grandma Elsie, do you know where Gracie is?"

"I think you will find her in the playroom."

Lulu immediately resorted thither and found Gracie playing happily with her dolls.

"Oh, Lu, I'm glad you have come!" she cried, glancing up at her sister as she entered.

"I do miss you so all day long while you are at school! But what's the matter with your hand?" she asked with concern.

"Nothing very serious," Lulu answered carelessly. "That villain of a music teacher snapped his pointer on my fingers and blistered them—that's all."

"Oh, Lu, what a shame! Did it hurt very much?"

"Quite a good deal, but of course it was the insult, not the pain that I cared for."

She went on to give the details of the occurrence to this new listener, who heard them with tears of sympathy and indignation."

"I think somebody ought to whip him," she said. "And I hope he'll never have a chance to strike you again, Lu."

"I don't intend he shall. I've said I won't take another lesson from him, and I don't intend to. But Grandpa Dinsmore says I must, so there'll be another fight."

"Oh, Lu, don't!" cried Gracie in terror. "Don't try to fight him. Don't you remember how he 'most made Grandma Elsie die when she was a little girl, 'cause she wouldn't do what he told her to?"

Lulu nodded. "But I'm another kind of girl," she said. "And I'm not his child, so I think he wouldn't dare be quite so cruel to me."

"How brave you are, Lulu!" Gracie exclaimed in admiration. "But, oh, I am so sorry for you! I'd be frightened 'most to death, I think—so very frightened to think of going back to that signor and dreadfully afraid to refuse if Grandpa Dinsmore said I must."

"Yes, you poor, little thing! But I'm not so timid, you know. Grandpa Dinsmore can't frighten me into breaking my word."

"But, you know, Lu," said Max, coming in at that moment, "that papa has ordered us to obey Grandpa Dinsmore, and if we refuse we are disobeying our father, too."

"I am sure papa never thought he would want me to go on taking lessons from a man that struck me," cried Lulu indignantly. "Besides, I've said I won't, and nothing on earth shall make me break my word, Max."

"I wish papa was here," sighed Max, looking sorely troubled.

"So do I," responded Lulu. "I'm sure he wouldn't make me go back to that hateful old Signor Foresti."

That evening Max, Lulu, Rosie, and Evelyn were in the schoolroom at Viamede, preparing their lessons for the morrow, when a servant came up with a message for Lulu. She was wanted in the library.

Flushing hotly, and looking a great deal disturbed, Lulu pushed aside her books and rose to obey the summons.

"Only Miss Lulu? Nobody else, Jim?" asked Rosie.

"I 'spects so, Miss Rosie. Lulu—dat's all Massa Dinsmore say."

"Oh, Lu, I'm sorry for you!" whispered Evelyn, catching Lulu's hand and pressing it affectionately in hers.

"You're very kind, but I'm not afraid," Lulu answered, drawing herself up with dignity. Then she hurried to the library, not giving herself time to think what might be in store for her there.

She started with surprise and paused for an instant on the threshold as she perceived that Professor Manton was there with Mr. Dinsmore, who was the only other occupant of the room.

"Come in, Lulu," Mr. Dinsmore said, seeing her hesitation. "You have nothing to fear if you are disposed to be good and docile."

As he spoke he pointed to a low chair by his side.

Lulu came quietly forward and took it.

"I am not afraid, Grandpa Dinsmore," she said in low and even tones. "Good evening, Professor Manton."

"Good evening," he replied with a stiff nod. "I am sorry to be brought here by so unpleasant a duty as laying a complaint against you."

"You needn't care. I don't," she said with the utmost nonchalance.

He lifted his eyebrows in astonishment and had nearly forgotten his dignity so far as to utter a low whistle but caught himself just in time.

Mr. Dinsmore frowned darkly.

"What is the meaning of such talk?" he inquired. "If you do not care for the displeasure of teachers and guardians you are indeed a naughty girl."

He paused for a reply, but none came, and he went on. "Professor Manton has brought me a report of your conduct today agreeing substantially with the one given by yourself, and I have called you down to tell him in your presence that you are to go on taking lessons of Signor Foresti."

Lulu's cheeks crimsoned, and she looked from one to the other with flashing eyes.

"Grandpa Dinsmore and Professor Manton, I have said several times, and I say it again. I will never take another lesson from that man!"

"Then you defy the authority of both the professor and myself?" Mr. Dinsmore queried sternly.

"In this one thing, I do."

"The consequences may be very unpleasant," he said significantly and with rising anger.

"I know the consequences of giving up and taking lessons again from Signor Foresti would be very unpleasant," she retorted.

"Leave the room!" he commanded with stamp of the foot that sent Lulu's heart up into her throat, though she tried to appear perfectly calm and unconcerned as she silently rose and obeyed the order.

"Really the most amazingly impertinent child I ever saw!" muttered the professor. Then aloud, "What is to be done with her, sir?" he asked.

"She must be made to obey, of course," replied Mr. Dinsmore.

"Yes, yes, certainly. But what measure would you have me take to bring her to submission?"

"None; you will please leave all that to me."

"Then if tomorrow she refuses to finish that interrupted lesson, you would have me simply report the fact to you?"

"No, sir, even that will be quite unnecessary. She will tell me herself. I am proud to be able to say of her that she is a perfectly truthful and honest child."

"I am glad to learn that she has at least one virtue as an offset to her very serious faults," observed the professor, dryly. Then, rising, "Allow me to bid you good evening, sir," and with that he took his departure.

Mr. Dinsmore saw him to the outer door, then returning, began pacing the floor with arms folded across his chest and a heavy frown on his brow.

Presently Elsie and Violet came in, both looking anxious and disturbed. Horace stopped his walk, and he sat down with them and reported all that had passed during the call of Professor Manton—after which they held a consultation in regard to the means to be taken to induce Lulu to be submissive and obedient.

"Shall we not try mild measures at first, papa?" Elsie asked with a look of entreaty.

"I approve of that course," he answered. "But what shall they be? Have you anything to suggest?"

"Ah," she sighed. "It goes hard with me to have her disciplined at all. Why will she not be good without it, poor, dear child!"

"Let us try reasoning, coaxing, and persuading," suggested Violet, with some hesitation.

"Very well," her grandfather said. "You and your mother may try that tonight. If it fails, tell her that so long as she is rebellious all her time at home must be spent in her own room and alone."

"Dear grandpa," Violet said pleadingly, "that punishment would fall nearly as heavily upon Gracie as upon Lulu—and a better child than Gracie is not to be found anywhere."

"Yes, yes, and it is a pity. But I don't see that it can be helped. It is a hard fact that in this sinful world the innocent have very often to suffer with the guilty. You are suffering yourself at this moment, and so is your mother, entirely because of the misconduct of this child and that fiery little Italian."

"Lulu is extremely fond of her little sister," remarked Elsie. "So let us hope the thought of

Gracie's distress if separated from her may lead her to give up her self-will in regard to this matter. Take courage, Vi; all is not lost that is in danger."

Each of the two had a talk with Lulu before she went to bed that night, using their powers of argument and persuasion but in vain. She stubbornly refused to be taught by Signor Foresti.

Violet was almost in despair. She was alone with the little girl in her dressing room.

"Lulu," she said, "it will certainly give great distress to your father when he learns that you have become a rebel against grandpa's authority. You seem to love your papa very dearly. How can you bear to pain him so?"

"I am quite sure papa would not order me to take another lesson of a man who has struck me," was the reply in a tremulous tone, which told that the appeal had not failed to touch the child's heart. "I do love my father dearly, dearly, but I can't submit to such insulting treatment. And nothing on earth will make me."

"You are not asked or ordered to do that," Violet answered gently. "The man is to be utterly forbidden to ill-treat you in any way.

"Perhaps I should hardly try to hire you to do right, but I think there is nothing I would refuse you if you will do as grandpa bids you. What would you like to have which is in my power to bestow—a new dress—a handsome set of jewelry—books—toys? What will you have?"

"Nothing, thank you," returned Lulu coldly.

"I will double your pocket money," came Violet's next offer, but Lulu heard it in silence and with no relaxing of the stubborn determination of her darkened countenance.

"I will do that and give you both dress and jewelry besides," Violet said with a little hesitation, not really feeling sure that she was doing quite right.

Lulu's eyes shone for an instant, but the stubborn look settled down on her face again.

"Mamma Vi, I don't want to be bribed," she said. "If anything at all would induce me to do as you wish and break my word, love for papa and Gracie and Max would do it alone."

Violet sighed. Drawing out her watch, "It is past your bedtime," she said. "Lulu, dear," and she drew the child caressingly toward her, "when you say your prayers tonight will you not ask God to show you the right and help you to do it?"

"Mamma Vi, it can't be right to tell a lie, and what else should I be doing if I went back to Signor Foresti for lessons after I've said over and over that I never would again?"

"Suppose a man has promised to commit murder. Should he keep that promise or break it, Lulu?" asked Violet.

"Break it, of course," replied Lulu. "But this is quite another thing, Mamma Vi."

"I'm not so clear about that," Violet answered seriously. "In the case we have supposed, the promise would be to break the sixth commandment — in yours it is to break the fifth."

"I'm not disobeying papa," asserted Lulu, hotly.

"Are you not?" asked Violet. "Did he not bid you obey my grandfather while he is not here to direct you himself?"

"Yes, ma'am," acknowledged Lulu, reluctantly. "But I'm sure he never thought your grandpa would be so unreasonable as to say I must take lessons from a man like Signor Foresti who had struck me — and that when I did not deserve to have it done at all."

"Lulu," said Violet in a frustrated tone, "your father made no reservation. But now, good night," she added in a more affectionate tone. "I trust you will wake tomorrow morning in a better frame of mind."

"But I won't," muttered Lulu as Violet left the room and retired to her own. "I'll not be driven, coaxed, or hired."

CHAPTER NINETEENTH

For what I will, I will, and there's an end.

— SHAKESPEARE

SHORTLY AFTER BREAKFAST the next morning and before the hour for setting out for school, Elsie called Lulu aside, and in a gentle, affectionate way asked if she were now willing to do as directed by Mr. Dinsmore.

"Grandma Elsie," said the little girl, "I am ready to do anything he bids me if it is not to take lessons of that horrid man who dared to strike me after being told by Grandpa Dinsmore himself that he must never do so."

"I am grieved, my child, that you have no better answer than that to give me," Elsie said. "And I think you know it will not satisfy my father. He will have those committed to his care obedient in everything. And he bade me tell you that if you will not submit to his authority in this matter—if you do not today obey his order to finish that interrupted music lesson—you must, on returning home, go directly to your own room and stay there. And as long as you continue rebellious, all your time at home is to be spent in that room and alone."

She paused for a reply, but none came. Lulu sat with eyes cast down and cheeks hotly flushing, her countenance expressing both her anger and her stubborn resolve.

Elsie sighed involuntarily.

"Lulu, my child," she said, "do not try this contest with my father. I warn you that to do so will only bring you trouble and sorrow. He is a most determined man, and because he feels that he has right on his side in this thing, you will find him unconquerable."

"I think that is what he will find me as well, Grandma Elsie," replied the determinedly self-willed little girl.

"Surely you are showing scant gratitude for the many kindnesses received at my father's hands," Elsie said. "But I will not upbraid you with them. You may go now."

Feeling somewhat ashamed of herself, yet far from prepared to submit, Lulu rose and hastened from the room.

She knew nothing of what had passed between Mr. Dinsmore and Professor Manton after her dismissal the night before, and it was with a quaking heart that she entered the schoolroom at Oakdale that morning.

Though in fear and dread, she had not the slightest intention of abandoning her position in regard to the music lessons.

Nothing, however, was said to her on the subject till the hour for meeting the signor. Then Miss Diana directed her to go and finish her lesson of the previous day. Upon receiving a refusal, she merely remarked that it should be reported to her guardians, and her punishment left to them.

Evelyn gave her friend an entreating look, but Lulu shook her head, then fixed her eyes upon her book.

As they drove home to Viamede in the afternoon, Gracie was waiting for them on the veranda there.

"Oh, Lulu," she cried as the latter came up the steps, "mamma has been helping me fix up my baby house and it is so pretty! Do come right up to the playroom and see it."

"I can't, Gracie," Lulu answered, coloring and looking vexed and mortified.

"Why not?" asked Gracie in a tone of surprise and keen disappointment.

But before Lulu could reply, Mr. Dinsmore stepped from the door and inquired, "What report have you to give me, Lulu?"

"I have not taken a music lesson today, sir," she answered a little coldly.

"Were you not told to do so?"

"Yes, sir."

"And you did not choose to obey? You know the consequence. You must go immediately to your room and stay there alone during the hours spent at home until you are ready to obey."

Lulu assumed an air of indifference as she walked slowly away, but Gracie burst into tears, crying, "Oh, Grandpa Dinsmore! You won't keep me, her own sister, away from her, will you? Oh, please don't. I can't do without her."

"My dear little girl," he said soothingly, taking her hand in his. "I am truly sorry to distress you so, but Lulu must be made obedient. She is now in a very rebellious mood, and I should do wrong to indulge her in it."

"Grandpa Dinsmore," she said, pleadingly with the tears streaming over her face, "I'd be frightened 'most to death if I had to take lessons of that cross, bad man. How can you make poor Lulu do it?"

"Lulu is not the timid, little creature you are," he said, bending down to kiss her forehead. "And I am sure is not really afraid of the man—nor need she be after what I have said to him about striking her or any of the pupils I send him."

"It'll be a long while before she'll give up," said Gracie. "Maybe she never will. Mayn't I go and talk to her a little and bid her good-bye? You know it's 'most as if she's going far away from us all."

She ended with a sob that quite touched Mr. Dinsmore's heart. Also he thought it possible that her grief over the separation from Lulu and her entreaties to her to be submissive and obedient might have a good effect. So after a moment's cogitation he granted her request.

"Thank you, sir," said Gracie and hurried upstairs to her sister's door.

"Please, Lu, let me in," she cried. "Grandpa Dinsmore said I might come."

"Did he?" returned Lulu, admitting her. "Well, it must have been altogether for your sake, not a bit for mine—his heart's as hard as stone to me."

"Oh, Lu, dear Lu, don't talk so. Do give up, so we won't be separated!" cried Gracie, throwing her arms round her sister and giving her a vigorous hug. "I never can do without you, and don't you care to be with me?"

"Of course I do," said Lulu, twinkling away a tear—for they were raining from Gracie's eyes now, and her chest heaving with sobs. "And it's just the cruelest thing that ever was to separate us!"

"But they won't if you'll only give up, and Grandpa Dinsmore says that horrid man sha'n't strike you again."

"Grandpa Dinsmore is an old tyrant!" said Lulu. "Nobody but a tyrant would want to force me to put myself in the way of being again treated in the cruel and insulting way Signor Foresti has treated me once already. And I won't go back to him, not if they kill me!"

"But oh, Lu, think of me!" sobbed Gracie. "Max can see you and talk with you every day, going and coming in the carriage, but I'm afraid I won't see you at all."

"Oh, Gracie, I have a thought!" exclaimed Lulu. "Ask Mamma Vi if you mayn't ride back and forth with us every morning and afternoon. There's room enough in the carriage, and the rides would be good for you. You'd have to ride alone one way each time, but you wouldn't mind that, would you?"

"Oh no, indeed!" exclaimed Gracie, smiling through her tears. "It's a bright thought, Lu. I'll ask mamma, and I'm 'most sure she'll say yes, she's so good and kind."

Violet did say "yes," making one condition only—that neither her mother nor grandfather should object.

They did not, and every morning and afternoon Gracie was ready in good season for her drive to and from Oakdale.

The other children were glad for her company, and as by common consent always gave her the seat next to Lulu.

For two weeks those short drives yielded the sisters all the exchange they had. They met with a warm embrace in the morning just before stepping into the carriage and parted in the same way on their return to Viamede in the afternoon. Then

Lulu went directly to her own room, shut herself in, and was seen no more by the other children till the next day.

During that fortnight the confinement and solitude were her only punishment. Her meals were brought to her and consisted of whatever she desired from the table where the family were seated. Also, books and toys were allowed her.

Every night Violet and Elsie came, separately, for a few words with the little girl—always kind, gentle, loving words of admonition and entreaty that she would return to her former dutiful and docile behavior. But they were always met by the same stubborn resolve.

At length one evening, she was summoned to Mr. Dinsmore's presence—in the library as before. She was again asked if she were ready to obey. On answering in the negative, she was told that, such being the case, she was to be sent to Oakdale as a boarding scholar and not to return home at all until ready to give up her willfulness and do as she was bidden.

She heard her sentence with dismay but resolved to endure it rather than submit.

"I'm not ready to break my word yet, Grandpa Dinsmore," she said with a lofty air "And perhaps Oakdale won't be a worse prison than those the martyrs went to for conscience' sake."

"Lulu," he said sternly, "do not deceive yourself with the idea that you are suffering for conscience' sake. A wicked promise—a promise to break one of God's commands—is better broken than kept. The sin was in making it."

"I don't know any commandment that says I must take lessons from Signor Foresti or obey somebody who has no relation to me," returned Lulu, trembling at her own temerity as she spoke.

"You are an extremely impertinent little girl," said Mr. Dinsmore. "And you are not altogether honest in pretending such ignorance. You know that you are commanded to obey your father, and that he has directed you to be obedient to me in his absence. I have ordered you to take lessons from Signor Foresti."

He paused a moment, then went on. "If tomorrow you do as you are ordered, you will be at once restored to favor and all the privileges you formerly enjoyed in this house. Otherwise, you will not return from Oakdale with the others in the afternoon."

He waved his hand in dismissal, and she left the room full of defiance—a most unhappy child.

In the hall she halted for a moment and glanced toward the outer door. A sudden impulse moved her to run away. But what good would that do? Where could she go? How would she find shelter, food, clothing? And should she ever see father, brother, sisters again?

She moved on down the hall and slowly climbed the broad stairway leading to the one above.

Violet met her there and felt her heart sink as she glanced at the sullen, angry countenance. She stopped, laid her hand kindly on the child's shoulder, and said, "Lulu, dear, I know pretty well what you have just been told by grandpa, and, my child, it distresses me exceedingly to think of you being sent away from us all."

"You needn't care, Mamma Vi. I don't," interrupted Lulu, angrily. "I'd rather be away from people that ill-treat me so. I only wish I could go thousands of miles from you all and never, never come back."

"Poor, dear, unhappy child!" Violet said, tears trembling in her beautiful eyes. "I know you cannot be other than miserable while indulging in such wrong feelings. If I have ill-treated you in any way, I have not been conscious of it, and I am truly sorry—for it is my strong desire to be all that I should to my husband's dear children. Come into my dressing room and let us have a little talk together about these matters."

She drew Lulu into the room as she spoke and made her sit on a sofa by her side.

"No, Mamma Vi, you have never ill-treated me," answered Lulu, her sense of justice asserting itself. "But I think Grandpa Dinsmore has, and so I'd rather go away from him."

"I am sorry you feel so little gratitude to one who has done so much for you, Lulu," Violet said, not unkindly. "Surely you cannot deny that it has been a very great kindness for him to take you into his own family—giving you the best of homes—and instruct you himself—for no reward but pleasure of doing you good and seeing your improvement. And he has done all that, too, in spite of having to bear with much ill-behavior from you."

Lulu tried hard to think herself unjustly accused, but in her heart she knew very well that every word of Violet's reproof was richly deserved. She made no reply but hung her head, while a vivid blush suffused her cheeks.

There was silence in the room for several minutes, then Lulu said, "I think my bedtime has come, Mamma Vi. May I go now?"

"Yes, good night," said Violet, bending down to give her a kiss.

Lulu returned both the kiss and the good night, then rose to leave the room.

"Stay a moment, dear," Violet said in her gentlest, sweetest tone. "I am writing to your father. What shall I say about you?"

"Anything you please," Lulu answered coldly and walked away with head erect, cheeks aflame, and eyes flashing.

"If she wants to tell tales on me, she may. I shan't stop her," she muttered to herself as she went into her own room and closed the door. Then sending a glance around upon all the luxury and beauty of the apartment, the thought flashed painfully on her that these things, so delightful to her, would have to be exchanged for others far inferior and less enjoyable, for, of course, no boarding school room would be furnished at anything like the expense that had been lavished upon this and others in this fine, old mansion—so long owned and at times occupied by the possessors of vast wealth joined to refined and cultivated taste.

During the last fortnight, enforced confinement there had sometimes made the room seem like a prison, but now her heart swelled at the thought of leaving it—perhaps never to return. Certainly, unless she became submissive and obedient, she would be kept at the academy at least until the family were ready to leave for Ion.

Then it occurred to her that there were advantages, companionships, and luxuries to be given up—the resigning of which would be still harder. Now that she was to leave them, she found she had grown fond of both her young stepmother and the baby sister of whom she had once been so jealous, and that she loved Grandma Elsie also and Aunt Elsie, too. Indeed, she found that almost every one in the family connection had proved agreeable in such exchanges as she had held with them.

Alas! What a sorry exchange from their society to that of the Mantons. To go from all the loving care that had been bestowed upon her and the many privileges accorded her at Ion and Viamede to the neglect and indifference to be expected from strangers! As she thought of all this she could not contemplate the carrying out of her sentence of banishment to Oakdale with anything like satisfaction.

Yet the idea of submitting to what she considered Mr. Dinsmore's tyranny being still more repugnant to her, she resolved to abide by her decision, risking all consequences.

She rose early the next morning and busied herself for some time in gathering together such books and toys as she wished to take with her. Then, seeking her young stepmother, "Mamma Vi," she asked, "am I to pack my trunk myself?"

"You are quite resolved to leave us, then, Lulu?" Violet inquired.

"I am quite resolved never to take another lesson from Signor Foresti," returned Lulu doggedly.

Violet sighed. "I had hoped you would wake this morning in a better mood," she said. "No, you need not pack your trunk. Agnes shall do it under my supervision. But it shall not be sent till the return of the children from school this afternoon, as I still hope to see you with them."

Gracie, who was present, stood listening in pale and wide-eyed astonishment.

"What is it all about?" she asked in alarm. "Is Lulu going away?"

"Yes," Lulu answered for herself. "Grandpa Dinsmore says if I won't take lessons from Signor Foresti, I must stay at Oakdale as a boarding scholar."

"Oh, Lu, Lu! Do give up and come back home," entreated Gracie, bursting into tears. "I can't do without you. You know I can't!"

Lulu drew her aside and whispered sweet words of comfort.

"It can't be for very long, I think, Gracie, because we'll be going back to Ion in two or three months. Besides, we can see each other every day, if you keep on coming in the carriage as you've been doing."

"But it will be only for a few minutes, and you won't have a bit of a nice time there."

"No, I suppose not, but even if it's pretty hard, I'd rather stay there than give up to that old tyrant."

"Please don't say that," pleaded Gracie. "I love Grandpa Dinsmore."

When the carriage came to the door promptly after breakfast, and the children trooped down ready for school, Grandma Elsie joined them on the veranda, wishing them a happy and profitable day at their studies.

Then, putting an arm about Lulu, she said to her in an undertone, "Lulu, dear child, I want to see you here with the rest tonight. You are one of my little girls, and I would not have you so rebellious that you must be shut out of my house. There! You need not answer, dear—only remember that Grandma Elsie loves you and longs to see you good and happy."

"Thank you, ma'am. You're very good and kind," Lulu said a little tremulously then hurried into the carriage—Max giving her the help of his hand.

The others were already in, and as Max took the only vacant seat by Lulu's side, he noticed that her face was very red, and that Gracie was crying.

"What's the matter?" he asked, glancing from one to the other.

"Lulu's not coming home with us tonight. She's going to board at Oakdale, she says," sobbed Gracie.

"Is that so? What for?" asked Max, looking at Lulu.

"Because Grandpa Dinsmore says I must, if I won't take lessons from Signor Foresti."

It was news to Evelyn, Rosie, and Walter as well as Max, having heard nothing of it before. There was a moment of surprised silence, broken by Rosie.

"Well, you may as well give up. Grandpa Dinsmore is not to be conquered, as I knew when the contest began."

Max and Evelyn were looking much distressed.

"Oh, Lulu, do!" entreated the latter. "You surely have held out long enough."

"I should think so, especially considering how kind Grandpa Dinsmore has been to us, and that papa ordered us to be obedient to him," Max said.

"I'd give up," remarked Walter. "'Cause there's no use fighting grandpa. Everybody has to mind him. Even mamma never does anything he asks her not to."

"The very idea of not being your own mistress, even when you're a grandmother!" exclaimed Lulu rather scornfully.

"Mamma is her own mistress," retorted Rosie. "It is only that she loves grandpa so dearly and thinks him so wise and good that she prefers to do just as he wishes her to."

CHAPTER TWENTIETH

Let come what will, I mean to bear it out.

—SHAKESPEARE

"THE HOUR FOR YOUR music lesson has arrived, Miss Raymond," announced Miss Manton.

Rosie and Evelyn both looked entreatingly at Lulu, but scarcely raising her eyes, she simply said, "I shall not take it today, Miss Diana."

"Very well, young lady. You will have to abide the consequences of your refusal," returned Miss Diana severely.

"Is it so very dreadful to live in this house with you?" queried saucy Lulu.

"What do you mean by that impertinent question?" asked Miss Diana, facing round angrily upon her.

"I only wanted to know in time," said Lulu. "What you said just now sounded as if you thought so—for that is the consequence I'll have to abide if I continue to refuse to take my music lessons."

"It shall be about as unpleasant as I can well make it in return for your impudence," was the furious rejoinder. "Also, you will remain in your seat during recess today."

"Oh, Lulu," whispered Evelyn at the very first opportunity. "It was not at all prudent to say what you did to Miss Diana. She will have it in her power to make your life here very uncomfortable or very pleasant if you don't take care."

"Yes," Lulu said with indifference. "I expect to have to pay for the pleasure of speaking my mind, but if she makes me uncomfortable, I'll manage to make her so, too."

As the hour drew near when the school would be dismissed for the day, a servant came in with a message. She said a few words in a low tone to Miss Diana, who at once turned to Lulu, saying, "You are wanted in the parlor, Miss Raymond."

The child's heart beat quickly as she rose and obeyed the summons but quieted when, on entering the parlor, she found Elsie and Violet its sole occupants. They had always been gentle and kind to her, and she loved without fearing them.

They made a place for her on the sofa between them, and taking her hand in a kind clasp, Elsie said, "We have come to take you home, dear child, if you are now ready to be good and obedient."

"I didn't take the lesson, Grandma Elsie, and I don't intend ever to do it as long as I live," Lulu answered in even, steady tones. "It was very kind of you and Mamma Vi to come for me, but I shall have to stay here till Grandpa Dinsmore gives up asking such an unreasonable thing of me."

"Then, Violet," Elsie said, "nothing remains for us but to see that she has comfortable accommodations and leave her here."

At this moment Mrs. Manton came hurrying in with profuse apologies for not having come sooner, but through the negligence of the servant, she had been until this moment kept in entire ignorance of their arrival.

"No, you must not blame the servant," Elsie said. "She acted by my directions. We wished to see this little girl alone for a few minutes and not to disturb you, knowing that you are busy with your pupils at this hour of the day."

"Ah! Then perhaps I am intruding," and Mrs. Manton drew herself up with dignity.

"Oh no, not at all," Elsie returned pleasantly. "Our private interview with the child is at an end. She is now to be placed here as a boarder—as you may perhaps know. And, if you please, we would like to see the room she is to occupy."

"Certainly, Mrs. Travilla. She can have her choice of several—or you the choice for her," Mrs. Manton replied, graciously leading the way as she spoke.

"You would like to come, too?" Elsie inquired, holding out a hand to Lulu.

"Yes, ma'am, thank you," Lulu answered, slipping hers into it.

They were shown several large rooms—intended and furnished for from four to six occupants each—two others of somewhat smaller size—which Mrs. Manton called double rooms—and one little one over the hall, which she said Lulu could have to herself if she liked that better than sharing a larger one with a schoolmate.

To Lulu's eyes it looked uninviting enough—so small, furnished with only one window, a single bed, one chair, bureau, and wash stand of very plain, cheap material. It was somewhat the worse for wear, and there was just a strip or two of carpet both faded and worn.

"I think this will hardly do," Violet said gently. "Have you nothing better to offer, Mrs. Manton?"

"No room that the young girl can have to herself," was the cold, offended reply. "Excuse me for saying so, but I think it is quite good enough for so obstinate and rebellious a child as I have understood she is."

"I am quite of your opinion, Mrs. Manton," said a familiar voice behind them. And turning, they perceived that they had been joined by Mr. Dinsmore with Professor Manton bringing up the rear.

Lulu was growing very red and angry.

"But she is my husband's child, grandpa," urged Violet quietly.

"And I am quite certain he would say she deserved nothing better while she continues obstinate in her rebellion against lawful authority," he answered firmly.

Lulu flashed an angry glance at him.

"It is no matter," she said. "Papa will set things right when he comes. And, Mamma Vi, don't be troubled about it at all. I shall tell him it was no fault of yours."

"No," Mr. Dinsmore said, smiling grimly. "I shall not share the responsibility. My shoulders are quite broad enough to bear it all."

Violet drew Lulu aside when they had all gone downstairs again, and with her arm about her waist, pleaded tenderly, affectionately with her to give up her rebellion and go home with them.

"We will start in a few minutes now," she said. "And, oh, dear child, I don't want to leave you behind. I shall grieve very much to think of you all alone in that miserable little room. Does it not seem a poor place after those you have had at both Ion and Viamede?"

"Yes, Mamma Vi, I have an idea that it's a good deal like a prison cell, but what do I care for that? I'd despise myself if I could give up just for that."

"No, dear, not for that, but because it is right to do it."

"'Tisn't worthwhile for you to trouble yourself to urge me any more, Mamma Vi," Lulu said loftily. "I am fully resolved as ever not to break my word."

"Then good-bye," Violet said with a sigh and a kiss. "You are not to be ill-treated—I settled that question with grandpa before we came. And if anyone should attempt to ill use you, let me know all about it at once."

Elsie, too, kissed Lulu in bidding her good-bye, but Mr. Dinsmore simply took her hand—given with evident reluctance—and said he was sorry to be compelled to banish her from the family circle, and if she willed it so, restoration of comforts and privileges of home would not be long delayed.

Lulu followed them out to the veranda, expecting to see the family carriage there with the other children, including her sister Gracie, but she was very sorely disappointed to perceive that it had already driven away.

A smaller one, which had brought Mr. Dinsmore and the ladies, was still there, and she saw them enter and watched it drive away till it was lost to sight among the trees.

Then a sudden sense of almost utter loneliness came over her, and rushing away to a secluded part of the grounds, she gave vent to her feelings in a storm of tears and sobs.

But by its very violence it soon spent itself. In a few minutes she became quite calm, did her best to remove the traces of her tears, and went back to the house, reaching it just as her trunk arrived.

It was carried at once to her room, and she followed to unpack and arrange her clothes in the drawers of the bureau and washstand.

There was no closet, and she found herself much cramped for room. It was very disheartening—for she loved neatness and order and perceived that it would not be an easy matter to maintain them here, where it was so difficult to find a place for everything and keep it there.

The supper bell rang, but she delayed obeying the summons in order to finish the work at hand. She was hardly more than five minutes behind time, yet received a sharp reprimand from Professor Manton and a black mark.

Of course she was angry and indignant and plainly showed that she was—not mending matters in the least thereby.

In sullen displeasure she took the seat assigned her and, glancing over the table, was tempted to turn away in disgust.

The food provided was of the plainest, scant in quantity, inferior in quality, and neither well prepared nor daintily served. All of which presented a striking contrast to the meals that Lulu had been accustomed to sit down to at Ion and Viamede.

She ate but little—in fact, homesickness had nearly destroyed her appetite.

"What a miserable supper!" she remarked to a schoolmate when they had gone from the dining room and were gathered on the veranda for the short half-hour that intervened between the meal and the evening study hour.

"It was quite as good as usual," was the rejoinder in a sneering tone. "What did you expect? Do you suppose the Mantons don't want to make anything off us as boarders?"

"I hadn't thought about that at all," Lulu said with a look of surprise and perplexity.

Then after a moment's cogitation, "I suppose they do want to make all they can out of us, and that would be the reason there was so little on the table. But would it cost any more to have it cooked properly? The bread was both sour and heavy, and the butter so strong that I'd rather go without than eat it."

"Rancid butter is cheaper than sweet — both as costing less and going farther," answered her companion. "Good cooks are apt to be able to command higher wages than poor ones. Also, like butter, bread goes farther if it is unpalatable."

"But if it makes people sick?" Lulu said — half in assertion, half in inquiry.

"Of course, but the Mantons don't pay our doctor bills or support us in invalidism if it comes to that."

She walked away, and Lulu stood leaning against a pillar lost in thought — more homesick than ever.

The boarding scholars were all some years older than herself and did not seem to desire her companionship. In fact, they looked upon and treated her as one in disgrace, shunned her society, and almost ignored her existence.

The study hour over, they gathered in groups, chatting together on such themes as school girls find most interesting. One or another now and then looked askance at Lulu, who sat at a distance, lonely and forlorn, watching them and half-envying their apparent merriment and lightheartedness.

How she longed for Evelyn, Gracie, and Max—even Rosie and the grownup people at Viamede!

It was a long evening to her. She thought the hands of the clock had never before moved so slowly.

At nine a bell called them all into Professor Manton's schoolroom where he read a chapter from the Bible and made a long prayer in a dull, monotonous tone that set most of his hearers to nodding or indulging in suppressed gapes and yawns.

It struck Lulu as a different service as conducted by him from what she had been accustomed to under the lead of her father or Mr. Dinsmore. They had always shown by tone and manner that they esteemed it a solemn and a blessed thing to read the words of inspiration and draw near to God in prayer—while this man went through it as a mere matter of form of no more interest than calling the roll at the opening of school.

The service was followed by a formal goodnight, and the pupils scattered to their rooms.

"The bell will tap in half an hour, Miss Raymond, and at the first sound every light must be instantly extinguished," Miss Diana said harshly, as she gave Lulu her candle.

"But what if I have not finished undressing?" Lulu asked in dismay.

"Then you will be obliged to finish in the dark."

"There won't be time to write in my diary, and I'll have to say my prayers in the dark," Lulu said to herself as she hastened up the stairs and into her closetlike apartment.

"What a forlorn bit of a place it is!" she grumbled half aloud. "Oh, it is so different from my pretty rooms at Ion and Viamede! Oh dear, oh dear! I wish that horrid Signor Foresti was back in his own country. I'm glad he doesn't live in this house, so I'd have to see him every day. It's bad enough to have to stay here without that. But I don't mean to let Grandpa Dinsmore find out how bad his punishment is. No, nor to be conquered by it either."

She had set down her candle and was hurriedly making ready for bed.

On creeping in, having blown out her candle just as the signal sounded, she discovered a new reason for regretting her change of residence. She must sleep—if she could—on a hard pallet of straw, instead of the soft, spring mattress she had been accustomed to rest upon at home.

She uttered an exclamation of both disgust and impatience, fidgeting about in the vain effort to find a comfortable spot and sighing wearily over the hard hills and hollows.

How Mamma Vi and Grandma Elsie would pity her! Probably they would say she must have a better bed, even if it had to be sent from Viamede.

But then Grandpa Dinsmore might put his veto upon that, saying, as he had that day in regard to the room, that it was quite as good as she deserved. And she would not give him the chance. She would put up with the hard bed and with all the other disagreeables of the situation, nor give up in the very least about the music lessons.

The situation seemed no brighter or cheerier the next morning. There was no one to give her a smile, a kiss, or so much as a pleasant word. Breakfast was no improvement upon last night's supper—Mrs. Manton scolded all through the meal—at her husband, daughters, pupils, servants. The professor bore it meekly as regarded her but was captious and irritable toward everyone else. Miss Diana looked glum and Miss Emily timid and ashamed.

The morning service that followed the meal was very like a repetition of that of the previous evening, and Lulu withdrew from the room after it was over, feeling less respect and liking than ever for the principal of the institution.

To her great joy the Viamede carriage drove up a full half-hour earlier than usual. Gracie alighting from it with the others and running to her said, "Oh, Lulu, I'm glad to see you! And I may stay till school time—mamma told me so. Grandma Elsie told Uncle Ben to bring us early and wait here for me till you go into school."

"It's very kind of them," returned Lulu, hugging and kissing her little sister. "And I'm ever so delighted to see you all," she added to the others who had gathered around her.

"And we to see you," Evelyn said, embracing her.

"What kind of time have you had?" asked Rosie and Max in a breath.

"About such as I anticipated," answered Lulu, nonchalantly. "Of course, it's not like home, but I didn't expect that."

She afterward, under a promise of secrecy, let Evelyn more into her confidence—described her bed, the meals, telling that she had learned from one of the older boarders that those she had partaken of were of average quality. She also told of the unpleasant manners of Professor Manton, his wife, and Miss Diana.

"Oh, Lu, it is quite bad that you should be exposed to such things!" said Evelyn. "Do give up to Grandpa Dinsmore and go home with us tonight!"

Lulu shook her head decidedly.

"Well, than, at least let me tell your mamma or Grandma Elsie about the hard bed. They will surely see that a better one is provided for you."

But Lulu negatived that also. "I can stand it," she said. "And I wouldn't for a great deal let Grandpa Dinsmore know what a hard time I am having. He would triumph over me, and say it was just what I deserved."

So no complaint was made, and Evelyn was the only person at Viamede who had any idea of the many discomforts Lulu was enduring for her own self-will's sake.

Sunday morning came, and Lulu made herself ready for church, all the time fearing that she would have to go with the Mantons and sit with them and their boarding scholars.

Great, then, was her joy on seeing Max drive up in a light two-seated carriage—Violet and Gracie on the back seat and a vacant space on the front beside the young charioteer.

"Oh, they've come for me!" cried Lulu, glancing from the window of her room. "How nice of Mamma Vi to do it!" and she flew down to the front door to greet them.

The professor was there before her, bowing, smirking, and asking in his most obsequious tones if Mrs. Raymond would be pleased to alight and walk into the parlor.

"Thank you, no," Violet said. "We have come merely to pick up Lulu and take her to church with us. Come, dear," to the little girl. "The professor will help you in, if you are quite ready to go."

"Yes, Mamma Vi," Lulu answered eagerly, and with the aid of the professor's hand quickly climbed to her place.

"Mamma Vi, you are very good," she said as the carriage rolled on again.

"Yes, isn't she?" said Max. "She says she isn't at all afraid to trust me to drive her."

"No," said Violet, smiling affectionately on him. "You do great credit to Uncle Ben's teaching. I think your father would be very much pleased with your proficiency, Max."

"Were you expecting us, Lulu?" asked Gracie.

"No, indeed! How should I when nothing had been said about it? But oh, I was so glad to see you coming down the drive."

The children seemed happy in being together again and chatted cheerily, Violet occasionally joining in.

She had fully gained their respect and affection, and they now never felt her presence the slightest damper upon their enjoyment of each other's society.

On their return, while yet at some little distance from the academy, Violet asked, "Lulu dear, do you find yourself quite comfortable and happy at Oakdale—so that you wish to continue there as a boarder?"

"I wish that rather than to go home again on Grandpa Dinsmore's conditions," Lulu said with a frown, and with that the subject was dropped.

CHAPTER
TWENTY-FIRST

Woes cluster; rare are solitary woes:
They love a train, they tread each other's heel.

—*Young*

FOR A NUMBER OF WEEKS events moved on their even course at Viamede. They were all well and happy, though Lulu's continued obstinacy caused most of them more or less mental disquietude.

She still remained at Oakdale, making no complaint to anyone but Evelyn of her fare or accommodations. She was studious and well behaved in every respect, except that she steadily refused to have anything whatever to do with Signor Foresti.

She had attended church regularly with the family, had seen all of them occasionally on weekdays, but had not once been permitted to visit Viamede, Magnolia Hall, or the parsonage.

If either she or Mr. Dinsmore regretted having begun the great struggle that now appeared so interminable, no one else was aware of the fact.

Gracie had kept up her habit of driving over to Oakdale every morning and afternoon, and the pleasure of seeing her often had helped Lulu greatly in the endurance of her exile—as had also her daily exchanges with Max, Evelyn, and Rosie.

But one morning in March they came without Gracie, and all looking grave and troubled.

"Where's Gracie? Why didn't she come?" asked Lulu with a vague feeling of uneasiness.

"She's sick," Max answered, trying to swallow the lump in his throat and keep the tears from coming into his eyes. "So is the baby, and the doctor—Cousin Dick Percival—says that both have the scarlet fever in its worst form."

Lulu, who knew something of the deadly nature of the disease, stood speechless with surprise and dismay. The other two girls were crying now.

Presently Lulu burst out vehemently, "I must go home! I will go! It's the cruelest thing in the world to keep me away from my darling Gracie when she's so sick and may be going to—oh, I can't say it! I can't bear to think it!" and she began sobbing as if her heart would break.

Evelyn put an arm about her.

"Lu, dear Lu, don't be so distressed. The doctor has not said that either case is hopeless, and they may both get well."

"The dear baby, too!" sobbed Lulu. "Oh, I do love her. She is such a darling!"

"Indeed she is," said Max, vainly trying to steady his tones. "And it's hard to see her suffer. Gracie, too—she's so sweet and patient and so good. I heard some of the servants talking together this morning about her, saying she was just like a little angel, and too good to live. And—and I'm afraid she is."

He quite broke down with the last word.

"No, she ain't," cried Rosie. "She's just as good as they think her, but good children are not any more likely to die than bad ones. Everybody that knew mamma when she was a child says she was as good as she could be and see how long she has lived."

"That's true, and I'm obliged to you for reminding me of it, Rosie," said Max, looking a little relieved.

"But I must go home now," repeated Lulu. "Gracie is sure to be wanting me, and I can't stay away from her."

"No," the others said. "None of us are allowed to go into the room for fear of the contagion. Indeed, we're not to go back to Viamede, but to stay at either Magnolia Hall or the parsonage till the danger is over."

"Mamma and Violet are nursing the sick ones with the help of Aunt Phillis," said Rosie. "Sister Elsie has gone to the parsonage with little Ned, and she and Isa will have to keep away from Viamede on account of their babies—so will Cousin Molly."

"Grandpa telegraphed for Cousin Arthur this morning. We know he is a skillful physician, and Gracie is begging for her own doctor."

"I'm glad. I hope he'll come quickly," said Lulu. "And oh, how I wish papa was here!"

"Yes, we always want our papa when we're in trouble," said Max. "We can't help feeling as if he could help us somehow. But perhaps it's a very good thing that he's not here just now to see his children suffer."

"Oh, are they suffering very much?" Lulu asked quite tearfully.

"Yes," answered Rosie. "Mamma told me they were both very ill—Gracie especially—her head aching badly, her throat distressingly sore, and her fever very high, but that she was sweetly patient under it all."

"I'm not surprised to hear that," sobbed Lulu. "She always was patient and good—never a bit like me. Oh, it is so hard that I can't be with her."

They were standing together in a little group on the veranda while they talked, and the agitation in their faces and voices had attracted attention from the scholars and teachers who happened to be within sight and hearing.

Miss Emily now drew near and asked in a kindly, sympathetic tone what was the matter.

Rosie answered, telling briefly of the serious illness of the two little sisters of Max and Lulu.

"Ah! I am extremely sorry," Miss Emily said. "You will find it difficult to give your minds to your lessons under such trying circumstances. I will go to my father and the others and ask that you may be excused if your recitations should be imperfect today."

"That was a kind thought," said Max, as she went into the house. "She's certainly the best and kindest of the family."

The ensuing week was one of great sorrow and anxiety to Violet, scarcely less than to her mother. The children were so dangerously ill that it was greatly feared both would succumb to the power of the disease.

It was a time of sore trial, but it brought out in strong relief the beauty and nobility of character in both Violet and her mother. They proved themselves the most devoted of nurses—patient, cheerful, hopeful, never giving way to despondency, or wearying in efforts to relieve the little suffers or wile them into forgetfulness of their pain.

Till the crisis was past they watched over them day and night, aided by Drs. Conly and Percival.

Arthur had obeyed with all possible dispatch, approved of what Dick was doing, and joined him in the care of the little patients. One or the other was always close at hand.

"This is a sad, anxious time for you, my dear Vi," Elsie said one evening as they sat together in the sick room—Violet with her deathly ill babe on her lap, while Gracie lay on the bed in an equally critical condition. "But you are bearing up bravely."

"Dear mamma, you help me very much in so doing," Violet said, low and tremulously. "So do Arthur and Dick. But best of all, 'underneath are the everlasting arms.' Oh, mamma, it seems as if my heart must break if either of the children is taken, and I may be called to part with both. Their father— my dear, dear husband—is so very far away."

She paused, overcome by her emotions.

"'God is our refuge and strength, a very present help in trouble,'" her mother whispered with a tenderly sympathetic look. "'He will never leave nor forsake you, dear child.'"

"No, mamma, my heart is constantly saying to Him, 'I have called thee Abba, Father! I have stayed my heart on thee. Storms may howl and clouds may gather—all must work for good to me.'"

"Yes, dear child," Elsie said with emotion. "'We know that all things work together for good to them that love God.'"

"My baby is so young, and Gracie is such a dear little Christian child, that, if I must give them up, I shall know that they are safe—'Safe in the arms of Jesus. Safe on His gentle breast.'"

Gracie, whom they had both deemed quite unconscious, opened her eyes and fixed them on Violet's face with a look of ardent affection.

"Yes, mamma," she said feebly. "I'm not afraid to die, because I know that Jesus loves me. My head aches. I'd like to lay it down on His breast. And— He'll comfort you and papa, and—the rest."

Violet could not speak for weeping, but Elsie bent over the child and, tenderly smoothing her pillow, said, "Yes, darling, He will, and whether we live or die, we are all His, and we know that He will do what is best for each one of us."

Gracie dropped asleep again almost immediately, and Elsie resumed her seat by her daughter's side.

"Oh," murmured Violet, "dearly as I love Gracie, I should far rather see her go than Lulu, because I am sure she is ready for the change, and I know their father would feel so, too. Mamma, how long it is since I heard from him! I begin to feel very anxious. Ah, what comfort and support his presence would be to me now!"

"Yes, dearest, but console yourself with the thought of how much anxiety and distress he is spared by his ignorance of the critical condition of these little ones. We may be able in a few days to write that they are better—out of danger with careful nursing, so that the news of their convalescence will reach him at the same time with that of their severe illness."

"Yes, mamma, there is comfort in that," Violet said, smiling through her tears.

On going down to breakfast the next morning, Elsie found her father seated at the table with the morning paper before him. He glanced up at her as she came in, and something in his expression of countenance set her heart to throbbing wildly.

"Oh, papa, what is wrong?" she asked. "My boys? Have you—? Is there bad news of them?" She quickly dropped down into a chair, trembling in every limb.

"No, no, daughter," he hastened to say. "I think they are all right. Here are letters from all three," pointing to a pile on the table before him.

She drew a long breath of relief. Then with another glance at his face, "But what is wrong? Certainly something is distressing you greatly. And Mamma is shedding tears," as she saw Rose furtively lift her handkerchief to her eyes.

"Yes," he sighed. "Something is wrong, and not to keep you in suspense—it is a report that Captain Raymond is lost. It is now some weeks since his vessel should have been heard from, and it is greatly feared that she has gone down with all on board."

"Vi! Oh, my poor Vi!" gasped Elsie. "Her heart may be overwhelmed. We must keep it from her as long as we can—at least till the children are better."

"Certainly," Mr. Dinsmore said. "My dear child," going to Elsie and taking her hand in his tender, fatherly fashion. "Remember it is only a report—or rather a conjecture—which may be without any foundation in fact. The captain may be alive and well at this moment."

A slight sound caused them all—Mr. and Mrs. Dinsmore and Elsie—to look toward the door opening in to the hall.

Max stood there—a face from which every vestige of color had fled, quivering with emotion.

"What—what is it about papa?" he asked hoarsely. "Oh, Grandpa Dinsmore, Grandma Elsie, don't hide it from me! I must know!"

"Max, my boy, how came you here?" Mr. Dinsmore asked in a kindly pitying tone, going to the lad and making him sit down, while he took a glass of water from the table and held it to his lips.

Max put it aside. "My father?—What about my father, sir?"

His tone was full of agonized inquiry, and Mr. Dinsmore saw the question was not to be evaded.

"My poor fellow," he said, "I am truly sorry you should be distressed by hearing what is as yet only a rumor. Fears are reported that your father's vessel is lost. But nothing is known certainly yet, and we must hope for the best."

For a moment the boy seemed utterly stunned, then, "I don't believe it! I won't believe it!" he exclaimed loudly. "We can't do without him, and God wouldn't take him from us. Would He, Grandma Elsie?" And his eyes sought hers with a look of anguished entreaty that she knew not how to withstand.

"My dear Max, I trust we shall have better news tomorrow," she said tenderly. "But whatever comes, we know that all things work together for good to them that love God. He is our kind, heavenly Father, who loves us with far more than an earthly parent's love, and will let no real evil befall any of His children."

"Yes, and—oh, I'm sure it couldn't be good for Lulu and me to be without our father to help us to grow up right."

No one present thought it necessary to combat that idea or show that it might be a mistaken one, since it seemed to afford some comfort to the boy.

"We will hope for the best, Max. Do not let these possibilities distress you." Mr. Dinsmore said kindly. "Come to the table and take some breakfast with us."

"Thank you, sir, but I couldn't eat," returned Max brokenly. "Grandma Elsie, how are Gracie and the baby faring?"

"I'm afraid no better, Max," she said in faltering tones. "The crisis of the disease has not yet come, but in regard to them also we must try to hope for the best. Indeed, whatever the result, we shall know it is for the best," she added with tears in her soft, sweet eyes. "Because 'He doeth all things well.'"

It was Saturday, and there was no school, but Max had promised Lulu that he would come over to Oakdale after breakfast and carry her the news in regard to the sick children.

She was extremely anxious and distressed about them. As soon as liberty allowed her to follow her inclination, she hastened to a part of the grounds overlooking the road by which he must come.

She had not been there long when she saw him approaching—walking slowly, dejectedly along with his eyes on the ground.

"Oh, they are no better," she said to herself. "If they were better, Max wouldn't hang his head down like that."

She stood still, watching him with a sinking heart as he came in at the gate and drew near her—still with his eyes cast down. And now she perceived that his countenance was pale and distressed.

"Oh, Max," she cried. "Are they worse?—dying? Oh, don't say they are!"

"No, they are no better, perhaps they may be tomorrow, but—"

He stopped. His eyes were full of tears as he lifted them for a moment to her face, his features working with emotion.

"Max, Max, what is it?" she asked, clutching at his arm. "Oh, what is the matter? You must tell me now, Max!"

"My father—our father—" He covered his face with his hands and sobbed aloud.

"Oh, Max, what about papa?" she cried wildly. "Oh, don't say anything has happened to him! I couldn't bear it! Oh, I couldn't! But I must know. Oh, Maxie, tell me what it is!"

She had put her arms round his neck and laid her cheek to his. He returned the embrace, hugging her tightly to himself.

"It mayn't be true, Lu," he said brokenly. "But, oh, I'm afraid it is. They say it's feared his ship has gone down with all on board."

"Gone down?" she repeated in a dazed tone, as if unable to believe in the possibility of so terrible a disaster. "Gone down?"

"Yes, in the sea—the dreadful sea! Oh, Lu, shall we ever see our father again in this world?"

"Do you mean that papa is drowned? Oh, I can't, I won't have it so! He'll come back again, Max—surely he will! I couldn't live without him and neither could you or Gracie. But, oh, maybe she will die, too! And I'm afraid it's because I'm so bad. God is taking away everybody I love, because I don't deserve to have them. I've been disobeying my father by not doing as Grandpa Dinsmore bade me, and now maybe I haven't a father to obey! Oh, Max, Max, what shall I do? Everybody's being taken away from me!"

"I'm left, Lu," he said, brushing away a tear. "I'm left to you, and you're left to me. We don't know certainly yet, that anybody is really taken from us, or going to be."

"Oh," she cried lifting her head, which had dropped upon his shoulder as he held her closely clasped in his arms. "I'll stop being so bad. I'll be good and do as Grandpa Dinsmore has ordered me, and maybe God will forgive me and spare papa and Gracie and the baby. Do you think He will, Max?"

"Perhaps. You remember how ill papa was when you were obstinate and disobedient to him once before, and you gave up and did as he bade you? Then, we all prayed for papa and he got well?"

"Yes, oh, yes. I'll do it now — this minute. I can't go to Viamede to tell Grandpa Dinsmore, but I'll write him a little note, Max, and you can carry it to him right now."

"I have a notebook in my pocket — pencil, too," he said, pulling them out in haste to get the thing done lest her mood should change. "I'll tear out a leaf, and you can write on that. Grandpa Dinsmore won't mind what kind of paper it is so long as the words are there."

He led the way to a rustic seat, tore out the leaf, spread it on the cover of the book, and handed that and the pencil to her.

"I needn't say much — need I, Max?" she asked, looking at him through tear-dimmed eyes.

"No, just the few words you would say if he were here beside you."

"I can't write nicely, my hand trembles so, and I can hardly see," she sobbed, taking her handkerchief and wiping away the fast-falling tears.

"Never mind. I know he won't care how it looks. He'll know why you couldn't do better."

Thus encouraged, Lulu wrote with her trembling fingers: "Grandpa Dinsmore, I'm very sorry for having been so naughty, so obstinate, and so disobedient. Please forgive me. I will do whatever you bid me, even if you still say I must take lessons again from Signor Foresti."

She signed her name in full and, handing it to Max, asked, "Will that do?"

"Yes, I'm sure it will, and I'm ever so glad you've done it at last, Lu."

"But, oh, Max, how can I go back to that horrid, little man after I've said so many times that I never would again?"

She seemed inclined to snatch the note out of his hand, but he stepped back quickly out of reach, hastily deposited it in the notebook, and that in his pocket.

"Don't repent of doing right, Lu," he said. "Think that you may be averting sorrow and bereavement. I think I'd better go now, Lulu, before you change your mind."

"Oh no, don't, Max," she entreated. "I'm so very lonesome without you. Let us keep together and comfort each other."

Max yielded, and they sat down again side by side.

Just then one of the schoolgirls came flying down the walk toward them, crying out half breathlessly as she drew near, "Lu Raymond, don't you want to hear the news?"

"What is it?" Lulu asked indifferently.

"Something you'll be glad to hear. You know the spring term closes next week. Well, it seems that the time of Signor Foresti's engagement here expires with it, and, as he had been offered a higher salary elsewhere, he refuses to renew the contract with Professor Manton. I overheard their talk. Something was said about you, and the signor remarked in a passionate tone that you had already missed your last chance to take another lesson from him, or even to finish that interrupted one. Now, aren't you glad?"

"Yes," Lulu said, a flash of joy illuminating her countenance but only to be instantly replaced by the very sad anxious expression it had worn before.

"Oh, Max, will Grandpa Dinsmore think I—?"

"No," interrupted Max. "I'll tell him all about it, and he knows you're honest as the day. Why," turning his head at the sound of approaching wheels, "there's Grandpa Dinsmore now! I'll run and tell him, Lu." Without waiting for a reply, he went.

"What's he going to tell?" asked the girl who had brought the news about Signor Foresti.

"That's our private affair," replied Lulu, coloring.

"Oh! Is it indeed?" and she walked off with an offended air.

Lulu was too agitated by contending emotions to care whether she had given offense or not. She sat still, watching from afar the interview between Mr. Dinsmore and Max. She saw the latter hand her note to the former, who took it with a pleased look, read it, said something to Max, then alighted and came toward her, Max accompanying him.

She watched their approach in some agitation and noticed that Max seemed to be talking fast and earnestly as they moved slowly onward.

At length they were close to her.

She rose with a respectful, "Good morning, Grandpa Dinsmore." Taking her hand in his, he bent down and kissed her, saying, "I am very glad, my dear, to be able to take you back into favor." He sat down on one side of her, Max on the other.

CHAPTER TWENTY-SECOND

Skies Brighten

"OH, GRANDPA DINSMORE!" cried Lulu with a burst of sobs and tears. "Do you think it's true that—that papa's ship is lost?"

"I hope it is not," he said. "Such reports have often proved false. So do not grieve too much over it. It is never wise to break our hearts over possibilities.

"But I know you and Max cannot help feeling anxious about both your father and your little sisters. That being the case, I do not think you can study to any profit. As the term has so nearly expired, I shall, if you wish it, take you away from here at once.

"Not to Viamede, of course, but to Magnolia Hall—Mr. and Mrs. Embury having sent you a warm invitation to make their house your home for the present. What do you say to my proposition?"

"Oh, Grandpa Dinsmore, how nice and kind of Cousin Molly and her husband!" exclaimed Lulu. "I shall be, oh, so glad to go away from here, especially to such a lovely home as theirs."

"Very well, then," he said with a smile. "Go and gather up your belongings while I settle matters with Professor Manton. Then I will drive you both over to Magnolia Hall—for Max is included in the invitation."

Lulu needed no second bidding but started up at once to obey.

"I'll go with you, Sis, and help you pack, if you like," said Max. The offer was accepted gladly. And as Mr. Dinsmore's business with the professor would take him to the house, all three walked thither together.

An hour later the children had bidden a final good-bye to Oakdale and were on their way to Magnolia Hall.

Arrived there, they received a warm welcome. Lulu was greatly pleased to find Evelyn a guest there also, and that they were to share the same room.

"Oh, Eva!" she cried. "I'm delighted that you are here. I thought you were staying at the parsonage."

"So I was," Evelyn said. "Rosie was here, but we exchanged. She and Walter have gone to visit Cousin Isa, while you, Max, and I let Cousin Molly entertain us in her turn. I find it simply delightful at both places."

"But, oh, Lu, how you have been crying! Is it about the sick little sisters?"

"Partly," Lulu answered, hardly able to speak for emotion. "They are still in great danger. But, oh, much worse than that! They say—that—that it's feared papa's ship is lost with—all on board. Oh, Eva, I've been so disobedient to my father for month's past, and now—I'm afraid I'll never, never see him again!"

Before she had finished her sentence, Evelyn's arms were around her, holding her close, while she wept with her.

"I can feel for you, dear," she sobbed. "I know only too well how dreadful it is to be fatherless, but it is only a report, which may be false. Do try to hope for the best. We will both pray for your dear father and for the little ones, that they may get well very soon."

After her long trial of the privations to be endured at Oakdale Academy, Lulu greatly enjoyed the comforts and luxuries of Magnolia Hall, but the suspense in regard to her father and little sisters was very hard to bear.

For two days longer there was no relief from that, but on the morning of the third, Max came bounding in on his return from Viamede. He had gone to make his usual inquiries about Gracie and the baby, and his face glowed with happiness.

"Oh, Lulu, good, good news!" he cried, tossing up his cap and capering about in the exuberance of his joy. "The children are considered out of danger if well taken care of, and we know they'll be that. Papa's ship has been heard from, too—all well on board. And we'll see him again, I do believe—perhaps before a great while!"

Lulu wept for joy. "Oh, I am so glad, so happy!" she sobbed. "But, oh, how I do want to see papa—the children, too! Can't I go to them now, Max?"

"No, not yet. They wouldn't let me go into the wing where they are. I mean the doctors wouldn't, because the danger of contagion is not over, and won't be for a week or more."

"So long to wait?" she sighed.

"Yes," Max said. "But we ought to wait very patiently, now that we have had such glorious news. And perhaps there'll be letters from papa for us by tomorrow."

His hope was fulfilled. The next morning's mail brought letters from Captain Raymond to his wife and each of his children—the baby, of course, excepted.

Max handed Lulu hers.

She almost snatched it from him in her joy and eagerness and hurried with it to her room, where she could be quite alone at this hour, Evelyn being at school. She was finishing out the term, not having the same reason for leaving before its close that ... and Lulu had.

But now that she held the precious, longed-for missive in her hand, Lulu could scarce find courage to open and read it. She had good reason to expect a severe reprimand from the father, whom, in spite of their mutual love, she had been persistently disobeying for the last three months. She would have given much to recall that past and feel herself deserving of his commendation and such words of tender fatherly affection as he had often addressed to her by both tongue and pen.

At last she tore open the envelope, spread out the sheet, and with burning cheeks and fast beating heart, read: "My little daughter, my heart misgives me that there is something very much amiss with you. Not sickness, for your mamma, Max, and Gracie all make casual mention of you. They say directly that you are well. Yet I have not seen a stroke of your pen for three months or more.

"Your little letters so full of 'love to papa' have been very sweet to me, so that I am loath to have them discontinued. Daughter, in addition to that, I have, as you know, directed you to constantly report your progress in your studies and your conduct. In failing to do so, you have been guilty of positive disobedience. What excuse have you to offer for such disregard of your father's commands?

"I cannot think there is any that will at exonerate you from blame. Now I bid you write at once, giving me as full and detailed a report of the past three months as you possibly can.

"My child, I love you very dearly. There is never a day, I believe, never a waking hour in which my heart does not go out in love to my darling Lulu. I always send up a petition to a throne of grace on her behalf. I think there is no sacrifice I would not willingly make for the good of any one of my dear children, and my requirements are all meant to promote their welfare and happiness in this world and the next.

"My child. My dear, dear child, your father's heart bleeds for you when he thinks what a hard battle you have to fight with the evil nature you have inherited from him!

"But the battle must be fought and the victory won if you would reach heaven at last.

"'The kingdom of heaven suffereth violence, and the violent take it by force.'

"You have a strong will, my Lulu. Make good use of it by determining that you will, in spite of every hindrance, fight the good fight of faith and lay hold on eternal life—that you will win the victory over your besetting sins, and come off more than conqueror through Him that loved us.

"I can hardly hope to hear that you have not been again in sad trouble and disgrace through the indulgence of your willful, passionate temper, and you will dislike very much to confess it all to me. You will be sorry to pain me by the story of your wrong doing, and certainly it will give me much pain. Yet I am more than willing to bear that for my dear child's sake. And as I have given you the order to tell me all and to refrain from doing so would be but a fresh act of disobedience.

"How glad I am to know that my little daughter is open and honest as the day! I repeat—write at once a full report to your loving father,

—Levis Raymond"

"Oh," cried Lulu, speaking aloud in the excitement of feeling. "I do wish papa wouldn't make me confess everything to him! I think it's dreadful hard! And what's the use when it hurts him so to hear it?

"And I'm sure it hurts me to tell it. I'll have to, though, and I won't keep anything back, though I'm terribly afraid he'll write that I must be sent away to some boarding school so that Grandpa Dinsmore won't be bothered with me anymore. Oh, dear! If papa could only be home, I'd rather take the hardest whipping he could give me. For though that's dreadful while it lasts, it's soon over. But he can't come now. They wouldn't think of letting him come home again so soon. So he can't punish me in that way, and I wouldn't take it from anybody else," she added with hotly flushing cheeks and flashing eyes. "And I don't believe he'd let anybody else do it."

She turned to his letter and gave it a second reading.

"How kind and loving papa is!" she said to herself, penitent tears springing to her eyes. "It's plain he hasn't been told a word about my badness—by Grandpa Dinsmore or Mamma Vi, or anybody else. That was good of them.

"But now I must tell it all myself. He says for me to do it at once, and I won't go on disobeying him by waiting—besides, I may as well have it over."

Her writing desk stood on a table near at hand, and opening it she set to work without delay.

She began with a truthful report of her efforts to escape becoming one of Signor Foresti's pupils and its failure, giving verbatim the conversations on the subject in which she had taken part. Then she described with equal faithfulness all that had passed between the signor and herself on the day of their collision and all that followed in the schoolroom and at Viamede.

She told of the fortnight in which all her time at home had to be spent in the confinement of her own room, then of the long weeks passed as a boarding scholar at Oakdale Academy. She described her bedroom there, the sort of meals served in the dining room, the rules that she found so irksome, and the treatment received at the hands of teachers and fellow-boarders. She repeated as she went along every conversation that she felt belonged to the confession required of her.

But the long story was not all told in that one day. It took several—for Lulu was too young and inexperienced in composition and penmanship to make very rapid work of it.

Evelyn was taken into her confidence. Captain Raymond's letter was read to her, then parts of the confession as it progressed from day to day, till she had heard the whole.

"Do you think I have told papa everything I ought, Eva?" Lulu asked when she had finished reading aloud the last page of her report.

"Yes, I can't see that you've kept back a single thing. I'm sure your father is right in saying that you are open and honest as the day! And, oh, Lulu, what a nice, good father he must be! I don't wonder his children all love him so dearly, or that you and Max were so distressed when that bad news came."

"No," Lulu said, hastily brushing away a tear. "But I am sure you must wonder how I can ever be disobedient to such a dear father, and I often wonder, too, and just hate myself for it.

"Now my report is ready. I'm glad it's done. It seems an immense load off my mind, but I must write a little note to go with it."

"Of course, you must," said Evelyn. "I'll run away and talk to Cousin Molly while you do it."

She hastened from the room, and Lulu's pen was again set to work.

"My own dear, dear papa, I have your letter—such a nice, kind one to be written to such a bad, disobedient girl. It came last Wednesday, and this is Saturday. Though I did obey you about the report, by beginning at once to write it, I had to make it so long that I couldn't finish it till now.

"I have tried to tell 'the truth, the whole truth, and nothing but the truth,' and Eva thinks I have succeeded in being faithful.

"Papa, I am really and truly sorry for having been so disobedient and obstinate—passionate, too, but I'm always being naughty and then sorry, then naughty again.

"I don't see how you can keep on loving such a bad child. But, oh, I'm glad you do, though it makes me sorrier than ever, and oh, so ashamed! I know I deserve punishment at your hands, and I have no doubt you will say I must be sent away to a boarding school. But, oh, dear papa, please don't! I do intend to be good and not give any trouble to

Grandpa Dinsmore or any of the rest. I think I was the first part of the winter and would have been all the time if they hadn't forced me to take lessons of that horrid man.

"Papa, I've always thought you wouldn't have said I must go back to him after he struck me. Would you? And don't you think Grandpa Dinsmore was very hard on me to say I must? I don't think anybody but my father has any right to punish me in that way, and I don't believe you would say he had.

"Dear papa, won't you please write soon again and say that you forgive me?"

That was not the whole of Lulu's letter. She had something to say of her own and Max's distress over the report that his vessel was supposed to be lost, of the sickness of the dear little sisters, and the pleasant time she was having at Magnolia Hall.

The letter and report together made quite a bulky package. Mr. Embury—not being in on the secret of the report—laughed when he saw it, remarking that "she must be a famous letter writer for so young a one." Lulu rejoiced when it was fairly on its way to her father but could not altogether banish a feeling of anxiety in regard to the nature of the reply he would send to her.

Gracie and Baby Elsie improved steadily till they were quite well and past the danger of a relapse.

All the members of the Viamede family gathered there again as soon as the physicians pronounced it entirely safe to do so. A week or two later, when the little ones seemed quite strong enough for the journey, they all set out on their return to Ion, where they arrived in safety and health. They received a joyful welcome from Edward, Zoe, other relatives and friends gathered for the occasion, the servants, and numerous dependants. And they found their own hearts filled with gladness in the consciousness of being again in their best-loved home.

The End